Bigger Than Jesus

Robert Chazz Chute

Bigger Than Jesus
By Robert Chazz Chute

Published by Ex Parte Press
Copyright 2012 Robert Chazz Chute
ISBN 978-0-9880082-4-3
First Edition: July 2012
Enquiries: expartepress@gmail.com
Cover design by Kit Foster of
KitFosterDesign.com

DEDICATION

This book is dedicated to J, C & C, who are all very understanding of my need to disappear into alternate realities and write my way back to my family, one word at a time. I have a hard time seeing what is right in the world, but because of these three, I never have to look far for a reminder of all that is right and good.

I am indebted to the most underrated American writer of the last century, William Goldman. People know him for *The Princess Bride* and his many movie scripts. They should know him for his many novels, as well. Mr. Goldman's writing style is a heavy influence on my work. The fast-paced style of Blake Crouch's *Run* also influenced me greatly in beginning The Hit Man Series. It's all about the next twist on the roller coaster track that you can't see coming.

My thanks go out to my editorial team/First Believers Club members: Janice Kurita, Peter Hawkins, Mark Victor Young, Johanna Goldenberg, Anita Martin and my weapons

experts, Brian Wright and RCMP Cst. Leland
Keane.

TABLE OF CONTENTS

COME TO JESUS

Water drips from the soot-black gargoyle's tongue like thin saliva, as if the grotesque statue is mocking you and eager for blood. Panama Bob Lima clings to the gargoyle, using it as a shield. You are on a thin ledge on the side of a very high building and for once you wish you wore your Nikes instead of twelve-hundred dollar Tanino Crisci shoes. So far, this job is not going at all as planned.

"You know this doesn't end well for you, either," Panama Bob says. "Oswald gets Kennedy and Ruby gets Oswald. The first rule of a conspiracy is to kill the assassin."

"They didn't give Ruby a choice. I don't have choices, either."

It's a long way down, so far that Tribeca's streetlights and cars swirl together in one red and white and yellow blur. Is your vision going whacky as a defence mechanism? Is your mind letting go so you can let go, black out and be blissful as you plunge into the concrete's existential abyss? What is it about telling yourself not to look down that makes you look down?

You should have told Big Denny to chase Panama Bob, but Denny's too fat to do much chasing. Instead, Denny De Molina guards the parking garage exit forty-something floors down and you're out here listening to Bob plead his case. The wind picks up and you feel light, like a sudden gust might pull you out into space. Denny's first clue that Bob is not escaping in his white Caddy could be you, bursting like a sack of meat on the sidewalk. Tonight could be your private 9/11.

It's not like you could refuse this job, but you should have stayed home, eaten a pot cookie with *SpongeBob* for company and given the mission a little more thought. The rain has made every surface slick. Panama Bob is talking fast and all those lights are starting to spin faster and it's hard to concentrate on what he's saying. You watch his mouth, as if you can read his thick lips. The vertigo recedes, though the sick feeling in your stomach remains. It would be very bad form, not to mention dangerous, to puke out here. This will be a crime scene in a few minutes. You swallow hard, choke back your gorge and focus on Panama Bob.

"C'mon, man. You know me. I'm as honest as can be."

True. Panama Bob is as straight a shooter as a high-stakes gambler and drug lord can be.

"Jimmy sent me, Bob. It's business. This is not personal."

"Excuse me, but killing me? I take that personal. Besides, I didn't steal from the company. I skimmed a bit, sure. We all do that, but I didn't steal."

"I understand what you're saying, Bob, but Jimmy Lima doesn't make those fine distinctions."

"C'mon, Jesus! I *made* you. Jimmy didn't want to let a Cuban in and I said to give you a shot. Now you're coming after me?"

"It was Big Denny who brought me into The Machine. I do feel bad about this, Bob, but Jimmy gave me a job to do. You know how it is."

How it is. It sucks is how it is. You're dizzy and the ledge is slippery and you wonder how long it will take you to plunge to your death? You think of the World Trade Center jumpers again. Technically, if it weren't for the attacks on September 11, 2001, you wouldn't be here at all. If not for those crazy terrorists, you wouldn't have watched the smoke from the twin towers rise up into the Tuesday morning sunlight from your apartment roof in Queens. You wouldn't have joined up in a vengeful fury. The plan was to earn your US citizenship — not just have it given to you — through military service. You planned to kill Osama bin Laden personally and collect the $10 million reward. You fully expected to get shipped straight to Afghanistan to go hunting.

Instead, you guarded a checkpoint outside the Green Zone in Iraq. Then things went from bad to worse. You got your US citizenship, a broken ankle in boot camp, nearly blown up on several occasions and trained in a bunch of skills that did not translate well to civilian life. Then there was the incident with the Afghan civilians on your second tour, the sergeant who deserved his broken jaw and the dishonorable discharge you didn't deserve for breaking that jaw.

When you got back, you couldn't find a job. Then Big Denny got you a no-show job at a construction site and things got easier and worse at the same time. It's like you're on that wide, easy road to Hell your Army chaplain always talked about. And now you're on a high ledge trying to kill your boss's lying, stealing, murdering douchebag brother. Worse? You have to listen to him whine about it.

"Dude! Let's go back inside and talk about this. We'll go climb back in my office window, have a drink to settle our nerves and then we'll call Jimmy together. I promise we can get through this little tiff and solve this thing. Vincent is not going to like this one bit! It's Jimmy's idea, but it's you starting the power play. Vincent wanted us both as underbosses but Jimmy wants to be the only one. That's what this is really about. Divisions are not good for business."

You edge a little closer along the ledge. "This is me following orders. I don't know what Vincent will say about your high-dive suicide. I just know that if I don't follow orders, Jimmy shoots me in the head."

"See, that's the difference between Jimmy and me. I'd never do that to you."

"And you won't have my car blown up tomorrow morning if I let you go? Yeah, right."

There's a thought. You should have blown up Bob's car. If you'd done that, you wouldn't be where you are now, rediscovering your fear of heights. At least when you rappelled from a helicopter in training it was over quickly and, when you threw up , all you had to do was endure the jeers of your platoon as your sergeant screamed at you for defiling his precious dirt.

Panama Bob is talking fast again, but you both know it doesn't matter. Jimmy sent you for Bob. That court takes no appeals, especially since Jimmy suspects Bob killed his personal bodyguard and best buddy, Cat Fornes. Martial arts fans remember Cat as a crazy, toothless cage fighter on TV. Big guy, big muscles, big yellow tiger tattoo that stretched from his neck to his feet and some mean jiu jitsu. His signature move was the spinning backfist. Cat might have been a champion except he got caught up in trying to use the backfist in every match so he'd have a brand. The other fighters caught on quick.

Jimmy loved Panama Bob like a brother, but he was a *fan* of Cat Fornes. You don't get to choose your family, but hooking up with a minor celebrity who had been on TV was more important to Jimmy Lima than any drug he ever sold. When Cat dropped out of the cage match game and came back to Queens, Jimmy made Cat a friend. Sometimes you wonder if he might have been more than that. The point is, Panama Bob may be a brother, but that's an accident of genetics and hormones and the back seat of a car. Jimmy loved Cat like the brother he *chose*.

When Cat went missing, Jimmy knew who to blame. Before Jimmy sent you for Panama Bob, he sent Cat to persuade the stolen money out of him. You stood in Jimmy's office when the underboss told Cat, "Bob's been skimming. Go have a talk with him. Show him that awesome spinning backfist and come back with the skim."

Bob might have weaselled out of this if their father was in the game. However, Vincent Daddy-O Junior, head of the family (father to Jimmy, step-father to Bob) doesn't know anything about all this. He's still laid out in a hospital bed recovering from getting his prostate cut out. This could blow up into a war and there's no good end in this for anyone.

Except maybe there is.

Bob holds up a key hanging from the fat gold chain on his neck. "Howzabout if I *bought* my way out of this? *You* could be out of this mess, Jesus. Don't you want to go back to Miami and be a wheel in warmer climes? Don't you want to be free of all this New York, New Jersey, rat race bullshit? "

You blink. "Tell me more."

"What I skimmed? It's in a storage locker."

"The money you said you didn't steal is in a storage locker."

"This is the key to that storage locker."

"Go on."

"Suppose I give you the location of this storage locker."

"And the key."

"Of course, *imbecil.* It don't work without the key."

"And you get to come in from the ledge."

"No. Big picture? *You* get to come in off the ledge, too. Everybody lives."

"Except Cat."

"I don't know what you're talking about."

"Sure. And how long before you think Jimmy finds us? A day? A week? What good is a sack full of money if I don't live long enough to spend it?"

Panama Bob is quiet for a minute. He looks down, gets a better grip on the gargoyle and when he looks at you again, he talks in a stage whisper, as if only you and God can hear. "There's enough, Jesus. There's enough there to run and hide for a long time. I was smart. I skimmed a long time and just took a little, but I was consistent. I wasn't greedy all at once. That's how they get you."

"Jimmy found you out."

"Not for years, Jesus. *Years!*"

"How much money are we talking about?"

"You'll never have to work again if you play it right."

"Yeah?"

"And you'll be living well. That sweet little señorita I seen you with in the club sometimes? Pete Vasquez's daughter?"

"Lily."

"You can play house forever and only stop for steak, lobster and oysters."

Hm. Lily *would* like that lifestyle very much. "And what are you going to do?" you ask.

"While you disappear, I'll be going to war. I was already making preparations when you showed up. I thought I had more time. I thought you'd come after me at home or something more discreet than hitting me at my own office. You kill Marv and Harvey? I didn't hear you throwing any shots, but when I heard your voice in the outer office I figured you'd come heavy and I climbed out here."

"I didn't have to throw shots," you say. "I just told your boys that Jimmy wanted to see them and that I'd do the babysitting. They went away."

"*Sonofabitch!* Fuckin' idiots!"

"Yeah."

Panama Bob looks up and blinks. The rain falls harder so you don't know if Bob is blinking away tears or water. The rain gurgles through the drains above you and the thin saliva from the big gargoyle's mouth builds to a little stream.

Readers Digest explained that the word *gargoyle* and *gurgle* come from the same language root. Somebody came up with the word gurgle from the sound the gargoyle made with the water going through it. That and movie trivia is the sort of crucial information that fills your head and kept you from learning anything useful so you could get an honest job. You're so stupid, you're wearing your shiny shoes with the too-smooth soles meant for office work and for show, edging along a tiny ledge, all the purchase in your toes. This is not what a smart ninja would do.

"Don't look down, Jesus," Panama Bob says. "Maybe you can walk on water, but you sure can't fly."

You think about Bob's skim for a full minute as the storm builds. The thunder rolls much louder out here, so close to the sky. You feel the boom in your chest and its force rivals your pounding heart. The first lightning flash strobes over Panama Bob and the gargoyle so, for a crazy second, they look like one grotesque, two-headed creature. Bob's got both hands wrapped around the gargoyle's neck, so his fancy nickel-plated .32 must be tucked into the waistband at the small of his back. He's no doubt still got a switchblade in his sock. You do, so why wouldn't he? Bob's got fast hands, too. That complicates things.

You inch back toward his office window. "Come inside before you get struck by lightning. You aren't any good to me if you're fried chicken."

Panama Bob's smile spreads ear to ear. "I knew you'd be a reasonable man. I know you!"

"I'm not reasonable, Bob. I just want out. With your skimmed milk, I can get away where Jimmy will never find me. At least for a while."

You almost slip. Almost. The smooth sole of your right shoe gives way and your heels dip. You throw yourself so hard at the wall you overcorrect and almost bounce off. You claw at the smooth wall and try to become part of it. You take another moment before you risk turning your head. Surprisingly, Bob is already around the gargoyle and coming up on you fast. When you glance down, you understand why he's so confident. His feet are bare. Bob moves along the ledge like he's climbing a shaky ladder: Cautious but in no real doubt he'll make it.

"I love these old buildings," Bob says. "Gargoyles! Can you believe it? Not only does it give the place character, so useful!"

"Yeah," you say as your left hand closes around the window frame to Bob's office. Bob's almost on top of you as you bend your knees and lean back, trusting the frame with your weight. Your right hand closes on Bob's calf, just below the knee. You miss the meat of the calf but you've got his pants leg and that's just enough. You drive with your legs so fast that you almost jump and Bob cries out as he twirls backward into the chasm.

If this were a Hollywood movie, he'd pull his piece from the small of his back and shoot in slow motion as he falls to his grisly death, the thick gold necklace and glittering locker key catching the city lights. In real life, he just has time for a short scream that cuts off with a bang as he careens into the concrete.

When you pull yourself through the office window, your legs and arms shake so badly you have to struggle to fish out your cell. "Denny! Get your fat ass up the ramp quick to the front of the building! Bob had a fall. Whatever's left of him is wearing a necklace with a key. Get that key off the body before the cops come!"

You don't wait for Denny's reply. Instead, you ransack Panama Bob's big desk. You don't have much time. Somewhere in this room there must be a receipt for a storage locker. When you find which storage facility is the right one, you and Lily are going to get away to fulfill some lovely dreams together.

That is, if the cops and Jimmy Lima and The Machine don't get you first.

THE KEY

You can't find the receipt for the storage locker in Panama Bob's desk. An ancient Underwood typewriter with black and white ivory keys sits on the desk. You lift it to see if a receipt is taped to the typewriter's bottom. Nope.

You thought you could be a cool and careful ninja about this and just roll the drawers out to find the receipt. Collect a zillion dollars. Do not go to jail. Instead, after a few minutes, all the drawers are dumped out on the floor and your hands are shaking.

Panama Bob wasn't such a bad guy, but he had no filing system you can discern. You wish Bob was less sloppy. If Bob had ordered you to hit his brother first, you'd be tossing Jimmy Lima's office now and you would have found the receipt already.

Jimmy's so anal, he changes three-thousand dollar suits to go from dinner to after-dinner drinks. Jimmy buys a new Beemer as soon as the new car smell fades on the old one. He uses a gold, jewel-encrusted lighter instead of a disposable one for $1.99. He's got a private courtyard under his bedroom window that's stuffed full of naked statues from Greece, all looking precisely east to greet the dawn with Jimmy as he drinks his morning espresso on his balcony. The coffee is the most expensive kind, the one with the beans that are eaten and then pooped out of a small animal before brewing.

The only items of interest in Panama Bob's desk are: one small baggie of green-brown weed, what appears to be the half-finished manuscript to the novel Bob was always tinkering with in his spare time and the nickel-plated .32 you thought he was going to use to shoot you out on the ledge. Sorry, Bob.

You call Denny on your cell. "You got the key?"

"Man, that was a mess."

"Yeah, yeah. That mess was almost me. You got the key?"

"Almost you?" The big bear sounds concerned. "You okay, buddy?"

"Better than Bob. Denny, if you don't tell me whether you got the key in the next two seconds, I'm going to throw myself out this fucking window."

"Got it. But he was—"

You don't need the details. You tell him to get out of the parking garage before the cops come. "Take your Dodge to the pizza joint around the corner and have a slice. I'll be there in a minute."

Big Denny's a mook. He's so big, he's fine for security gigs up front in a XXXL tee that's still too tight around the biceps. He's the bar bouncer who stops trouble just by showing up. However, in this situation, he's too hard to miss. He's not built for hanging around a crime scene.

Denny has been out of jail for more than two years — aggravated assault, but the other guy deserved it.

Considering Denny's muscles and tattoos, he always looks like a guy on day parole. A sharp cop might think to ask him what he was doing there. Denny could get himself into trouble talking to a cop about the weather. You're the one who handles the nuance, art and public relations required if anyone in a uniform needs some lies thrown their way.

It's a big building. When the cops show up they'll set up a cordon and question anybody who leaves the building. Time is spiteful and speeding up and your hands are shaking more as you rifle a filing cabinet. Instead of the storage locker receipt, you find porn magazines. Bob really did hate modern technology.

You don't have time to go through every book on Bob's shelves. If Panama Bob had come to you first, it'd be Jimmy drowned in the big fountain in the center of his mansion's circular driveway and you would have found the goddamn receipt by now. All of Jimmy's books are fake: all-leather bindings and each of equal height, as if he's some scrub ambulance chaser in a late-night infomercial begging to be a legal beagle for clients with lung diseases caused by bad insulation.

If you had Jimmy's money, you'd know what to do with it. If. You can give yourself an ulcer thinking about If.

If you were Panama Bob, where would you keep the receipt for the storage locker that holds your fortune? Your eyes settle on a framed picture of Jimmy and Bob on a boat. Panama Bob's got a big, goofy grin on his face and he's holding up a small fish. Jimmy stands behind him, toasting the camera with a martini glass. Only Jimmy would think to stock a deep sea fishing boat with olives and toothpicks and only Bob would consider a baby sailfish a prize. You took that picture. You find the safe behind the frame. You hadn't known Bob had a safe. Maybe he wasn't so goofy.

You peek out the window. In the street, a crowd gathers to gawk at the body. There's no time to get a sledge and hammer that little safe out of the wall.

You scoop up the phone from the floor and speed dial Jenny, the woman who still thinks she's Bob's ex-wife, not his widow. She answers on the third ring. You thought you might just piss yourself waiting through rings one and two.

"Hallo, Bob. What do you want?"

"Jenny, it's Jesus."

"Hey, *Hay-soose!*" She drags out the syllables, just to bust your balls, like that's original. She does that even when she's not drunk, which she is now.

"Jenny, I've got some bad news. Bob had a fall."

"Yeah? How is he?"

"Dunno. I haven't seen him yet. Jimmy wants me to check something in Bob's office safe. Do you know the number or know where I could find the number?"

"Nope. I didn't know he had a safe. Tell him to open it up and pay my alimony. He's behind by two months. I got bills, too. Tell him that."

"Shit."

"Anything else, *Hay-soose*?"

"What's Bob's birthdate? The doctor will want to know for their records."

She hems and haws and you resist the urge to start swearing at her. That would make you feel better, but it won't help. Finally, she says, "April 20, 1970. Hey, is Bob going to be okay?"

"No. No, he won't, Jenny. Sorry." And you really are.

You hang up and try spinning the dial on the combination lock. Past zero left to four, spin right to twenty, back left to 70.

When you try the handle on the safe door, it opens with a *chunk* sound. Bob was an idiot and you're a genius.

The safe is empty. You just joined Bob's Idiot Club.

Back to the window. There's a cruiser pulling to a stop with blue and white flashing lights and, even at night, you can tell there are upturned faces and pointing fingers. The police will "secure the scene" first, meaning they'll tell everybody to step back while they check on the body and dig out some yellow tape to rope off at least as far as the blood spatter. A shift supervisor will show up soon and they'll form a perimeter. That's what you would have done when you were an MP.

Once the perimeter is set up, you're trapped and trying to talk your way out. You've got to look like just another office worker on his way out after a hard day in a cubicle. You grab Bob's trench coat and umbrella on the way out the door and, after a moment's thought, you double back and grab his briefcase and sling the strap over your shoulder. In your suit and tie and briefcase, you look like another Joe Jobber. You take the stairs to the lobby.

You're almost out the back door when you realize you should have opened up the umbrella at the bottom of the stairs. High up in a corner, a security camera hangs from the lobby wall. Its red light blinks as it catches your movement and turns on, catching your mug perfectly. There's nothing you can do about that now so you hit the back door. The rain smacks the pavement so hard it bounces back up. Head down and hunching with cold water running down your neck, you open Panama Bob's umbrella and head for the pizza place.

Denny's got his face a couple inches from the table top, chewing the top of a loaded pizza. It's especially gross because he's not eating the bread. He takes your look and smiles wide, a dot of tomato sauce on his nose.

"New diet?"

"Low-carb. It's not so bad for you if you just order the works and eat the top but leave the bread."

Denny's last diet was all durian, all the time. Durian is an exotic fruit that smells like garbage. He stuck with that until he got the squirts and shit his pants running after a dealer for The Machine who was putting more up his nose than he was dealing. It's hard to be taken seriously as an enforcer if you lose bowel control while you're trying to have a serious conversation, even when you've got said deadbeat in a headlock.

"Is the low-carb thing working?"

"Down five pounds from three days ago," Denny says.

That five pounds must have come out of his feet because he looks just as fat as ever. "Yeah, I think I can see it in your face."

Big Denny smiles wider. It's safer to stay on the happy side of a felon who can crack walnuts with his hands. Denny saw Marlon Brando do that in that movie with Matthew Broderick and dedicated himself to the practice so much he's got early-onset arthritis.

When he hands you the key, you take a close look. Besides the number 408, there's no clue in which storage site Panama Bob's stolen fortune might be. This is New York. There must be a dozen such places close by. When the economy went south, lots of retail spaces emptied out and a bunch of them were turned into storage facilities. There's even a TV show about vultures bidding on storage lockers sight unseen so they can salvage the contents for cash. Before the recession, they wouldn't have all those lockers eligible for plunder.

"Too bad about Bob," Denny says. He's watching you carefully to see if you maybe need a hug.

"Anybody see you take the key from his neck?"

Denny nods. "Coupl'a homeless guys, sure."

"That's not so bad."

"And some tourists outside the coffee shop across the street from Bob's."

"Great." Your mouth goes dry so you look for the pizza waitress but she has disappeared. It's often difficult to get good service when you eat with Denny. He's too scary for most citizens. "How'd you know they were from out of town?"

"They stopped to watch after Bob went splat."

"Oh."

"And they didn't run away when I showed up. They just stood there with their mouths hanging open. Fucking tourists."

The red sauce is spread across his lantern jaw and his cheeks. It's like eating with a little kid, which, to you? Big Denny De Molina will always be a little kid.

"Congratulations," you say. "You just confirmed every stereotype the flyover states have about New York City."

Denny shrugs. "Gave 'em a story they'll repeat for generations." He tries to mimic a woman's voice and instead sounds like Miss Piggy. "This one time? My grandfather was in New York? You know...like dat."

He offers you a slice he's torn off. He surely hasn't washed his hands since he took the key from Bob's broken neck. It doesn't matter if it's fresh dead guy. He should have washed his hands before digging into pizza. Your stomach turns upside down and you thank him but shake your head.

"So will the cops think old Bob committed suicide? Jimmy wanted it to look like a suicide."

The desk drawers are spread everywhere. The safe door is hanging open. "Maybe," you say. "Or maybe they'll think it was a robbery. Hard to say."

"You gonna tell me what the key's about?"

You thought about this on the walk over so your next lie is already in the chamber, ready to fire. "There's a storage locker somewhere. I don't know where, but Bob tried to get me to let him go with the stuff in the storage locker." You lean in close, whispering even though no one else is in the place. "Bob had pictures of Jimmy's wife!"

Denny's forehead furrows. This is a total fabrication this time, but there's precedent for it. "Babs? No way!"

"Solid."

Denny startles and jumps and does a double-take like he's mugging in a silent movie. You get a sick look at Denny's gold tooth and the red ball of mush and pineapple in his maw.

His eyes narrow. "I thought she was past her younger, wilder days, man. Jimmy and her went through couple's counselling and everything. Jimmy screws around. That's expected, a man in his position. Lotsa business trips and whatnot. But Babs? I don't see that in her anymore. Especially not after what happened to the last guy."

"You never told me about the last guy."

"Long story, long time ago, before you came on the crew. Some things you don't want to know and I can't tell you since I don't get that drunk and sad anymore. It was one of those *Pulp Fiction*-type foot massage situations. The guy...old flame. Long before Jimmy. One time only thing. But he's still a missing person's case, you know what I mean? Jimmy walks in on them, *in flagrante delicious pussy*. Next thing you know, the guy's begging to get to be a missing person. You get me? If Babs was screwing around, she'd be...you know...discreet now. Really. Jesus. Brother. Dawg! Really! Who'd be that stupid as to sleep with Jimmy Lima's wife?"

You didn't think you'd get this much resistance from Big Denny. You improvise. "Barbara is still a good-looking woman. Total MILF material. I'm guessing it's Jimmy's computer tech guy. Freejack Jack lives in the guest house so he's there all the time and Barbara is out by the pool sunning herself. Next thing you know? Porn movie."

"Nah. Freejack's got no balls."

"What about the personal trainer guy who comes around the house for those private hot yoga lessons?"

"Chad?" He shakes his head. "Gay."

"Yeah, but maybe he's the kind of gay that's flexible about it. Any port in a storm, you know. Jimmy's wife could turn on the Pope."

Denny's eyebrows furrow and he looks twice as

scary. "This is...terrible news."

"We gotta find that storage place, man. And zip it until we know what's going on, for sure. Jimmy's not going to like this. We don't want him going off half-cocked and shooting Barbara in the face."

"No. We don't want that," Denny says. "What we going to do when we find those pictures?"

You shrug. "Once we know who we're dealing with, then we go to Jimmy with it. Maybe it's nothing. Maybe Bob was just blowing smoke so I wouldn't toss him off the building."

"Maybe." Denny brightens and returns to his pizza. "You really threw Jimmy's brother off the building, huh?"

"Well, it wasn't like Kevin Costner doing the bad Elliot Ness thing, throwing the guy off the rooftop in *The Untouchables*."

"How was it like?"

"Sort of like being Kevin Costner, only I almost crapped my pants and I had no hate for Panama Bob. It was just a thing I had to do, you know?"

"I know." Denny stretches out a paw and pats your hand. "Sorry, Jesus. I shoulda gone up myself. You know how you are with heights."

You went on the Ferris wheel at Coney Island once and almost threw up while waiting in line, but since you were on a date with Lily, you held it down and she thought you loved the Ferris wheel.

You reach inside the trench coat and your fingers close around a thick leather wallet. "I think I've had enough excitement for one night. Your dinner is on Panama Bob tonight, may he rest in peace."

"Pieces. Jimmy is okay with killing his own brother while the big boss is in the hospital? What you think he'll do to whoever's screwing Barbara?"

"Slow death. Vice grips and fire might be involved. Bad karma all around." You open the wallet and there's a bunch of the usual cards. You slip out the bills, a fifty and twenties and tens and count it out under the table. There's just over three-hundred dollars in your hands. You tell Denny it's about two-hundred bucks and give him half that before slipping the rest in your pants pocket.

While Denny trudges off to the bathroom to wash his face, you take inventory of Bob's wallet. There's a slip of paper with Chinese characters on it that's obviously from a fortune cookie. The English side reads: "You will be a great and persuasive writer."

You pull out a bent business card for a hair salon The Machine owns and a business card for Chad, Barbara's personal trainer. It's got a telephone number on it written in ink and "Chad" is written out in childlike, block letters. You hope Denny can keep his mouth shut so nothing bad comes Chad's way. He's not much more than a kid and, with that lisp and those lycra shorts, it's obvious that any violence that went his way would be unfair, collateral damage. You just need time to figure out which storage business is the right one so you and Lily can get away from this life and start a new one that doesn't require you to chase anybody out on high ledges in the rain.

Another business card catches your eye and this one's a surprise. The card advertises a jazz spot called Thackeray's Horn Club. On the back, in loopy, girly letters, someone had written "Melba." A telephone number with a prefix for cell phones sat cramped beneath the name. Whoever Melba was, she'd left a thick greasy lipstick kiss, now smeared, but no less visible in bright, do-me-quick red. Poor Panama Bob. He had hidden depths and lived fast until the pavement stopped him short. You plan to feel really bad for him later. *Push that thought away and save the grief for later.*

Denny punches you in the shoulder gently. "Jimmy called me while I was in the can. He says he wants a meet, right away, do not pass go."

You tell Denny you want to swing by your apartment first.

Denny shakes his huge head. "No time. When the Underboss calls, gotta go."

You want to ditch the key so it's not on you when you see Jimmy. You can talk in circles, but Denny's a straight line kind of guy and could blurt out something to make Jimmy suspicious. You trust Denny with your life, but not with a secret or to tell a solid lie.

Denny's like a brother. You almost want to tell him, "Sorry, man. No one's doing Jimmy's wife. I just told you that so I could keep all of Panama Bob's skim to myself." Almost. But half of a fortune might not be enough to get far away for a long time before The Machine finds you. Sure, Denny's like a brother, but Lily is *the one*, plus she sleeps with you. No contest.

You tell Denny you're still sick from the vertigo as you run to the bathroom. You pretend to throw up. Making lots of noise, you stand on the john and hide the key above a ceiling tile. You give it a few more minutes of theatrics before you come out wiping your mouth with your handkerchief.

The pizza girl is back behind the counter, looking worried about what she might have to clean up in the men's room. You ask for an extra-large decaf to go, "just to get the taste out of my mouth."

Then Big Denny's driving you to Jimmy's house and you're thinking that this is going to get deeper and darker before you see the light.

But if it all works out, you can get out of The Machine. Belonging to Lily would be different than being owned by Jimmy. Lily is the most gorgeous Latina in all of New York. Her love is the kind of slavery any man would choose gladly.

LOVE & NOOKIE

You know you're in trouble when Denny doesn't want to talk baseball. He's a Yankees fan and the easiest way to wind him up is to talk about the Mets. "Santana's going to be healthy in time for spring training. D'jou hear that?"

Big Denny shrugs.

Uh-oh.

The java is bitter and burns your tongue. You put the steaming coffee in the cup holder to let it cool. The meeting with Jimmy could go south in all kinds of ways. What does Jimmy want with you tonight? Bob's dead. Jimmy shouldn't want to be within 100 miles of you. He should be sending you to Atlantic City to let the heat ease. Your stomach feels like you swallowed an ice cube. What if the big boss, Vincent, is awake? He just had the prostate surgery today, but that old son of a bitch is tough. Maybe he's up and making decisions again from his hospital bed. Could Vincent suspect that Jimmy gave you the contract to take out Bob?

Jimmy is a hothead who made mistakes from the get-go. He told you to hit Bob at his office. "Send a message, but keep it away from his house on the Upper East Side. I paid off Bob's gambling debts and I paid the fucking mortgage on his overpriced house. I don't want any trouble turning around and selling it, what with blood smeared on the walls. That shit *stains*!"

Jimmy's second mistake was to send Denny with you. Denny's not ninja muscle. The third mistake? Jimmy said Bob would be alone. As soon as you walked into the outer office, there were Bob's guys, Harv and Marv. You had to improvise so you told them Jimmy wanted them to take the night off and you'd take over babysitting Bob.

That could be bad for you. Maybe Jimmy was wrong about those guys. Maybe they were more old school than new school and, when the reorganization happens, they'll stick with Vincent instead of Jimmy. You just killed the contender to the throne. The old man won't take kindly to you if he finds out you're the hit man. Not that Bob was much of a contender. As criminal masterminds go, poor Panama Bob would have made an okay fisherman.

What if, like Bob said, Jimmy's plan is to blame everything on you? Bob would be out of the way and Jimmy could go crying crocodile tears to Vincent about the Cuban outsider. Vincent is a smart guy, but a father suffering cold grief might order Harv and Marv to do some creative origami with your scrotum before he began to suspect his other, conniving son.

"Denny," you say, "I'm starting to think this might be a trap."

Big Denny's head jerks and he swerves right to pull into a construction lot by a black pit. You follow Denny's lead and open your door. You can't see the bottom of the hole and it looks like no one's around. Is Jimmy late or are Harv and Marv going to show up, shoot you in the back of the head and throw you in the hole?

The rain makes the car roof a snare drum and drowns out Big Denny. You lean closer to make sure you hear him right.

"Whaddayamean, Jesus?"

"I said, a *trap*. Like *Star Wars*...Death Star... General Akbar. It's a trap!"

"Explain."

You tell him Jimmy might be setting you up. Jimmy might be setting *him* up. "There's lots of hit men. Maybe not with my flair for fashion, but still, expendable. And you? No offense, dude, but to get more of you, all Jimmy has to do is snatch up the guys with bad knees who drop outta pro football tryouts who were supposed to play Special Team."

"Yeah. I gotcha. Where's the trap?"

"We're scapegoats, man. Jimmy blames us and gets the empire when the old man steps down. Vincent will retire in Boca to play golf and go to oncologist appointments and Jimmy will be king."

"I get it," Denny says. "You hand Jimmy the locker key and tell him who's screwing his wife and Jimmy will put it all on him. Whoever's screwing Jimmy's wife will take the fall for Panama Bob's hit and you're in the clear, Jesus." Big Denny smiles and you can see his gold tooth glint in the light cast up from the dashboard. "You're a smart guy, dude. You'll figure out which storage place that key belongs to and then Babs and her *lovuh*? They are *so* screwed."

"I hadn't thought of that."

"Christ, Jesus, if I thought about it, you must've.

You got that key. The key is the key to the whole thing." Then Big Denny De Molina, your brother from another beaver, balls up his fist and pops you hard in the face. Before you can say anything pithy about that, he pops you again.

You fumble for the open car door to get your balance in the soft mud. The pain is explosive when Denny hauls back and nails you square in the face again. You're propelled to your back. Bright raindrops flash through the glow cast by the streetlight and fall cold on your face. You're slow and your gears are disengaged. Denny hit you hard enough to push the clutch in your brain. *The raindrops fall from far above. If you were a raindrop, you'd stay high up where it's safe.*

You're still fumbling for your SIG Sauer when he lifts you off the ground and slams you down, knocking the wind out of you. "I'm the guy sleeping with Barbara, dawg! You playin' me? You think Big dumb Denny dudn't know what *time* the motherfucker *is*? Who would be stupid enough to mess with Babs? *I* would. Me! I fuckin' *love* her, dawg!"

How did you not see that? He looked you dead in the eye and asked who would be stupid enough to screw Jimmy's wife. Of course, there are lots of guys dumb enough. You might have caught on, but you thought you were just making it up. You had no clue he was doing Barbara.

He picks you up again. If he gave you time, you'd tell him it was all a ruse so he wouldn't want in on the skim. He won't believe you now, anyway. Besides, you can't move any air. Your nose is broken and spewing blood. Maybe those are raindrops or maybe they're stars.

He takes your pistol from your belt and tosses it through the open car door onto the driver's seat. You're still rolling around and grabbing your face, trying to get your lungs to work as he rips the switchblade from your sock. He checks your pockets. If you had the key on you, you'd be dead.

You're up in the air again and Denny's holding you in a bear hug from behind, his fists crushing into your solar plexus. You look down into nothingness. You're over the edge of the construction pit with nothing between you and the darkness but a flimsy yellow boundary tape flapping in the wind. It's a hole for a high-rise. It's a long way down. You try to focus on one good feeling. You tilt your head back to feel the cold wash down your forehead and open your mouth to drink a few drops of water. The rain tastes sweet. It's the last thing you will taste besides blood.

"Where's the *key*, dawg? Down in that pit, tomorrow morning, they're going to find you impaled on a bunch of rebar, maybe still dying but begging for the fire department to pull you off so you can die proper. You know what I'm sayin'? Stigmata ain't the half of it, *Hay-soose*! Where's the key? I hate to do this to you, brother, but for me and Barb's sake, I gotta get those photos!"

The blood from your smashed nose is running into your crumpled and soaked thousand-dollar suit. Your feet don't even touch the ground. You finally move enough air to laugh.

Until Big Denny squeezes tighter.

"It's back at the pizza place!"

"Bullshit!"

"Would I lie to my big bear?"

He throws you into the dirt like a broken doll. Your wrist scrapes raw and the elbows and knees on your suit are wrecked. *Armani!* Why couldn't Denny have had this tantrum when you were wearing the Hugo Boss with the stupid striped lining?

"If you're shitting me, dawg, it's you with rebar sliding through your guts. You get me that key and it's just a double tap behind the ear and sweet dreams."

You're up on your knees, scrabbling toward the yawning passenger door. The mud's turning softer and slides under you like you're trying to crawl up the down escalator. You hear a grunt as Denny bends to grab you by your belt, no doubt to slam your head into the side of the car. You feel that big paw making a grab for that fine python skin belt you bought at a flea market in Florida, but he fumbles the ball and you slip away.

You get one foot underneath you and you launch yourself at the car. You get some weight on the other foot and you're doing a Superman. You are flying, parallel to the ground. You crash land into the passenger seat.

Your SIG is close, waiting for you on the driver's seat. You almost have it when a vice circles around your left ankle and yanks you back. You struggle to dive for it again, but there's no traction in the mud giving way beneath you. You're half in and half out of the car on your knees when Denny wraps a big paw around your left elbow and flips you on your back, still half in and half out.

"Jesus, I'm sorry to do this to you, but you ain't gettin' in the way of love and nookie. You gotta ride in the trunk till you simmer down so we can go make sure that key gets safe in my pocket."

Denny grabs your legs and starts hauling you out.

You are not getting your gun. The hot coffee will have to do. You grab it from the cup holder and scald your hand as you squeeze to pop the top.

Big Denny sees it coming and stumbles back, but not before you splash it in his eyes. He's grabbing at his face and screaming, stumbling back and reaching for the pistol in the back of his waistband. You scramble up, push off from the side of the car and throw your shoulder into his big belly.

You almost slip in the mud again. You almost fall short of pushing him by a foot. Almost.

Big Denny has his gun out and would shoot you in the face, but the edge of the pit gives way under his heels and for one almost comical moment both the big man's arms pinwheel in the air, trying to grab traction from raindrops.

He falls back, out of the light, straight as a tree, down into darkness.

You collapse in the mud, gasping.

For the second time in an hour, you've thrown a man you liked from a great height. You could do this professionally.

RUN

You park Denny's ride around the corner from your apartment and go up using the service elevator. Maybe those tourists saw a well-dressed Cuban man fitting your description throw Panama Bob from his office tower and maybe they didn't, but the cops will have your picture from the security camera soon. Denny's either dead or bleeding out at the bottom of the construction pit. Worse, does Jimmy really want you to report to him, or was that just Denny's ruse to get you to the construction site? Is there already a contract out on you? Are you the goat in Jimmy's nasty power play to take over the Lima empire? These are the sort of nebulous complications that get a dude dead.

If you just barrel into your apartment, you're going to make a mess of the carpet and blood never comes out of shag. You put Panama Bob's briefcase on the tile floor along with the knife from your sock, your SIG Sauer, belt holster and the spare mags. You take your clothes off just inside the front door and leave the ruined black Armani jacket and pants on the tile. Everything aches and it seems to take a long time to accomplish what should be an easy task. It would help if you could breathe through your nose.

You stuff the suit, muddy and torn, into a green garbage bag. You'll miss that suit. Two gay salesmen at a clothing store fawned over you while Lily sat back with a cappuccino and giggled. She kept the salesmen busy running back and forth, fetching you more linen shirts and silk ties to try out. The ruined jacket didn't make you feel good because the fine cloth fit you perfectly. It made you feel charged because it reminded you of Lily in that store's leather chair. Her little black dress and high heels showed off her long legs. She pointed at each shirt and tie with long manicured nails, a large gold ring for every finger except the ring finger on her left hand. She sat, sipping cappuccino and laughing, directing the festivities like a queen. You so want to be her king, her jester and her slave.

In the six minutes it takes the hot water to kick in, you keep the cold shower spray on your nose, trying to numb it to the terrible throbbing. When the hot water winds its way up to your shower nozzle, you turn around and let the water pulse over your back and have a good cry. You can't remember the last time you cried, but this seems like the right time.

You learned English from Tia Marta, a German immigrant in Miami. It was Tia Marta who insisted you break the stereotype and assimilate like she did. "Don't say 'Chit!', little boy! Say 'Shit!' like a goddamn American." She started you out with the same books she learned English from: Mickey Spillane novels. None of Spillane's heroes would be very proud of you tonight. Mike Hammer never cried in the shower. But Hammer never got hammered by

Big Denny De Molina.

The hot water runs out and you shake through your core. You climb from the tub carefully and wipe the steam from the mirror to inspect your face. Your nose is swelling badly. Worse? It's not at the lovely angle you're used to. Your eyes point straight ahead, but your nose is looking off to the side in dismay.

"Dennis De Molina, the monster who was the closest thing I had to a best friend in all of New York City was such a slob, he never left things the way he found them," you tell your reflection. The pain is bad, but you're crying a little for him, too. With your nose broken, your voice sounds squeezed. You sound like a constipated duck.

Not long after 9/11, you found yourself at Fort Drum. At the end of your third week of Basic, you were on night maneuvers. The idea was to find another squad, camouflaged and hidden. The Drill Instructor didn't trust anybody with night-vision equipment yet, so the task was an exercise in working together, being thorough and not panicking. A little wrestling to get captured men back to your squad's flag was supposed to be the fun bonus. To amp up the tension of competition, if the other team eluded capture until dawn, it meant shit duty for your squad. You can't remember why that seemed to matter at the time because further experience proved that everything in the army was shit duty.

The DI didn't allow flashlights, either, so aside from the aforementioned "work together, be thorough, don't panic," finding the opposing team was really luck and moonlight. The guy in front of you was lucky, at least at first. He "found" one of the other squad by stepping on him. Your squadmate either panicked or was hyper-competitive because, when the guy popped up to run, he smashed the dude's face with the butt of his M4 carbine. Good thing no one was trusted with live rounds yet or the moron might have shot him.

"You fucking idiot!" The guy with the busted nose stepped close and kicked panicky guy right in the balls.

You could only make out the silhouettes' interplay, but it was your team member's sickened moan that turned your stomach. The guy with the broken nose sounded like a constipated duck. He continued to yell at the fallen man and kick him in the ribs to punctuate his cursing.

A DI appeared with a flashlight and asked you why you weren't helping your fallen teammate.

"Sir! Because my teammate is a fucking idiot, sir, and the guy with the broken nose is not kicking the shit out of my squadmate, sir!"

"He's not? Then what the hell is that man doing?"

"Sir! He is training my squadmate, sir!"

That got a laugh and the DI turned to the guy with the broken nose. "What is your damage, boy?"

The guy's nose was smushed to the side, just like yours is now. In the yellow circle thrown by the DI's flashlight, the recruit put one hand on either side of his nose and with one savage move, made it straight again. You heard his nose click into place, even over the sound of your teammate at your feet, vomiting.

The DI didn't blink because DIs don't blink. "Can you continue with this night exercise, son, or do you need a medic like this pussy rolling around on the ground is going to need?"

"Sir! This recruit can continue with the exercise,

sir!" He still sounded like a constipated duck, but less so.

"Well, then carry on, boy!" the DI bawled.

Before running off into the night, he turned to you, gave a cruel smile and kicked you in the balls, too. You doubled over in agony. The DI doubled over laughing. The guy with the broken nose had been a paramedic before the army. Later, he became an officer. You did not.

Back at the mirror: You try to set your own nose with one savage twist. It takes quite a few savage twists and more crying. You have to commit to the move, but every time you put your hands on either side of your nose to straighten it, the throbbing pain rises to a silent scream from prescient nerves. The anticipation of pain is so bad, you might start to believe in auras because even raising your hands in the vicinity of your face is enough to make your eyes water more. Was a watery eye okay with Mike Hammer? You can't remember, but surely even Mickey Spillane would allow his hero to get a bit teary with a badly broken nose. That's wrong. This nose is actually very well-broken.

You're stalling.

"In three...two...one...*nnnnnope*!" You pound your chest with one fist but when that makes your whole head throb, you think better of trying any macho bullshit to pump yourself up.

"In three...come on! In two...don't wimp out now! One, so I can be pretty again!"

Clunk!

Agony.

And you got a *clunk*. Why a *clunk*? Captain America-Kick-You-in-the-Balls got a *click*. Why did you get a *clunk*?

You breathe hard (through your mouth, of course, since a wad of bloody toilet paper is stuffed up each nostril.) When you dare to look in the mirror again you see that, yes, your nose is straight. The nose will be okay, though both eyes are going black fast. No problem, you tell yourself. Jack Nicholson got his nose sliced open in *Chinatown* and he solved the mystery or got the bad guys or whatever the hell he did in that movie. He probably didn't cry about it as much as you do now, but you've got a whole broken nose and his wound was just one cut.

You ruin a bathroom towel, the bathmat, a t-shirt and a tea towel in the kitchen waiting for the bleeding to stop.

You hear your apartment door slam and you figure Jimmy has sent Harv and Marv to kill you. That would be fine with you just now. When you look up, the lovely Lily Vasquez is upside down. You must have passed out a little because you're lying on kitchen tile, caught in the soft light from behind the open refrigerator door, ice cubes clutched to your face. You're on your back and Lily only *looks* upside down. You glance up her dress as far as you can see, and then begin the laborious task of righting yourself and making it to your knees.

She stands at the edge of your tiny galley kitchen, hands on hips and pissed. She surveys the geography of your face, one eyebrow quirked high. "Are you in trouble?" she asks.

"I don't know why you'd think that." Your voice sounds too high and nasal, but thankfully less duck-like.

"Jimmy Lima's looking for you and being rude to

me."

"Oh." You take a few centuries to form the next thought. Civilizations rise and fall while you cogitate and formulate. Oddly, she's still here when you finally manage, "I'm not sure about Jimmy. I think the Irish Mob might be after me."

"The Irish Mob?"

"Yeah," you say, slightly more swift now, gathering steam. Only one eon passes before you answer. "The Irish Mob. You know. As in...the cops."

"Get up."

"I'm not feeling altogether sexy right now, sweetie."

"Dead or alive, you're coming with me."

"A *Robocop* line? Now? Baby, you're my dream girl."

"Come with me if you want to live."

"That's definitely *Terminator*. And *Terminator 2*. And *Termin —*"

"Jesus, either get up and get going right now *before* the Spanish mob or the Irish mob busts in here or I'm leaving."

"You wouldn't leave me like this, would you?"

"With the mob or worse on the way? I'll get the hell out of here and I'll take your left nut in my clutch purse as a memory of all the wonderful times we had."

"Don't talk like that. Please."

"I thought you liked the dirty talk." Lily leans on the doorframe. No matter how she stands, Lily looks like she's in a glamour pose, like she should be stepping onto a movie screen or off a magazine cover.

"It's not the dirty talk that breaks my heart,

sweetie. It's you talking about us in the past tense. Can't have that."

She's one of those women who is beautiful when she's angry, though she's stunning when you make her smile. Smiling's better.

"Move faster, Jesus." She sweeps her bejeweled hands up and down her torso, "Or you'll never have this again."

You get your feet under you.

Move! Feel the pain but walk anyway and, no matter what, don't lose Lily.

MORE LIES FOR LILY

Lily gets you dressed and out of the apartment. You're all the way to the service elevator before you have to run back to the apartment to pull two more black Armani suits (still in their dry cleaning bags) from your closet and fish your go bag out from under the bed. Lily gives you the look when she sees the suits but she asks about the big backpack.

"My sergeant taught us a few phrases in Latin. *Non semper erit aestas.* It means be prepared for hard times and zombie attack. We've always gotta be zombie-ready."

"Jesus, you're delirious. How's your nose?" She reaches out to touch it and you flinch away. "If you're going to be a tough guy, keep in mind for next time that a bag of frozen peas or hash browns conforms to your face and works much better than holding ice cubes on your skin. I think you've got freezer burn on top of everything else."

"Sweetie, I'm such a tough guy, I got no frozen peas and no hash browns."

She pinches your nose and you shriek like a little girl. Well, not if the little girl was Lily. She tells you to squeeze the bridge of your nose to stop the bleeding. When you tilt your head back, you taste blood. Before you can bring your chin down, Lily slaps the back of your head. "Just pinch your nose. Don't let your head fall back or the blood will run down your throat! I swear, you throw up in my car, I don't care how bad you feel, you're cleaning it up!"

You step on the service elevator and ride down. Staring at the wooden planks, both of you are silent. By the time the service elevator's door opens, she lets you in on what happens next. "We'll go to my father."

"Pete works for Jimmy."

"He's my father more than he's a bookie. You get in trouble, you go to Dad."

"My dad was eaten by a shark, so I never got that." Still pinching your nose, you sound like a chipmunk's squeak muffled by heavy snow. "What's this about Jimmy insulting you?"

She shrugs. "I'm a big girl. I told you because it pissed me off, not because it's a problem for you to solve."

The rain has let up a little by the time you are out in the street and you think how great a night in the city smells after a hard rain. It's like all the sweat and stink and dirt gets flushed down the sewers and the air is cleansed. You have to think about it because you sure can't smell it. "I wonder if my smeller is broken forever. I'll miss your perfume most."

"That would be a shame," Lily says, but you detect no worry or warmth in her voice.

"I know what's up with me, babe. What's up with you?"

"S'up? Huh. Well, let's see. I get a call from my father's employer asking me for my boyfriend. He says you have been calling Panama Bob's ex and asking about a safe. He asks me where you are and, of course, I say I don't know. I tell him it's not like we're an item or anything. We just go dancing sometimes."

"You're saying we aren't an item?" Your head is beginning to throb again.

"I told him we're no item."

"Are you saying to me we aren't?"

"Baby." She reaches out to caress your cheek. "The way you're looking right now and the trouble you're putting me through? It's not a good time to ask that question."

"Ah."

Lily hits her key fob button, the Toyota beeps and the door locks click open. As she climbs behind the wheel, she reminds you not to bleed in her car.

"So Jimmy asks me straight out what's this about a safe and I say I have no idea and he says some rude things. No name-calling, you understand. Just hinting that maybe I know more than I'm saying and if that's true, he'd get hot about that. Then he says he was at my christening and my confirmation and tells me that good Catholic girls should listen to their parents and godparents and 'fess up before things get complicated."

"That doesn't sound rude."

"Oh, that wasn't the worst of it. Then he told me to give the phone to my father. Daddy listens and nods so hard, you'd think Uncle Jimmy can hear his brain rattling around in his head over the phone. Then Daddy tells Jimmy he'll have a talk with me as if I'm, like, six years old. As soon as he hangs up, he starts in on me."

"Did Pete hurt you?"

She throws you the first smile of the night and it is a sight to behold as the streetlights flash by. Her full lips pull back over pearl white, even teeth and she's all dimples. "Daddy talks big but he'd never lay a hand on me. I'm my mother's daughter. Any man lays a mad hand on me, he'll pull back a quivering stump."

You believe her and when you nod, the throbbing in your nose reminds you how hard Big Denny could hit. You wonder if your best friend is even now being slowly impaled on a grid of steel rods and praying for death. You'd feel bad and cry some more if that hadn't been what Big Denny had planned for you.

"I told Daddy that I'd find you and he wasn't so keen on that, you being you. But what Jimmy wants, Jimmy gets. That's his problem. He gets it all and still wants more."

"Did he say anything about Panama Bob?"

"Uncle Bob had a fall."

Yeah, he had a great fall. And all the king's horses and all the king's men...

"Is Uncle Bob going to be okay?"

Uncle Bob. Not a real uncle. Panama Bob is an uncle to Lily like Tia Marla was your aunt. Children adopt neighbors and family friends and strangers and sometimes even mafia bosses and call them uncle and aunt. Bob and Lily weren't close, but close enough that Bob came around with Christmas and birthday presents. Lily might not understand that you had to kill the guy who set her up with her Barbie collection, Malibu dream house and whatever that toy RV for Barbie was called. Lily might not understand that when Jimmy Lima tells you to kill somebody, you do it or somebody else gets the job but they have to kill you first.

"Jesus! I asked you a question."

"Uncle Bob is not going to be okay."

"I figured that much since you were asking about his safe." She lights a cigarette off the car's lighter and rolls down the window a couple of inches to let the smoke trail from her lips to the wind. Her father, Pete Vasquez, is the most successful bookie on the East Side. He's so sharp at his job, he gave her this car for her twentieth birthday. He's not so sharp that he knows she smokes yet. Or maybe she's just that much smarter.

"Where's your portly friend with the bad breath?"

"Denny's missing in action. Prolly killed in action."

She waits until the next red light for the next question so she can look in your face when she asks. "Did Denny De Molina murder my Uncle Bob?"

"Yup." It's close to the truth. Jimmy told you to kill Panama Bob and Denny drove. He knew the mission.

"Did you get Denny or did Bob?"

"I got Denny." You're squirmy over that truth, but rush to it so you can get back to being the hero.

"Shit." She pauses a moment after the light turns green and drives on, a little faster and weaving her way through traffic.

"Yeah," you say, thinking of how you had owed Big Denny for rent from when you first moved to the city. You never got around to paying him, but that debt is erased now, along with all the good things about Denny. Funny how he could be a badass and there were lots of things to not like about him, but it's the good stuff that makes you hate him more now. Each good thing about Big Denny De Molina demands that you feel bad. And you do, worse than about Bob. Bob was a job. Denny's dead because you lied to keep his big paws off Bob's skim.

"You said the cops are after you. Did they do this to you?"

"Nah. Denny gave me my facial redesign."

"Then he deserved to die," Lily says.

You get a warm feeling in the pit of your stomach.

"Twice over," she adds. "Once for self-defense and once for Uncle Bob."

Back to ice.

"The cops know you killed Denny?"

"Uh...no, too early, but they might have a witness I got to worry about." Another lie to Lily, though you guess you could call the camera eye a witness. You can't tell her which crime scene you were fleeing at the time. You can't be honest and still keep her. Without Lily, there wouldn't be much point in getting hold of all that storage locker money.

Heh. "Storage locker money." It isn't Panama Bob's skim or even Jimmy Lima's money anymore. It's storage locker money — money with no owner until you can get to it. You'll have enough money to get away with Lily and never look back on this shitty night. Or all the other shitty nights since Big Denny pulled you in and got you a job working for the Limas. You turn your head away from the lovely Lily, even managing to tear your eyes away from her long legs exposed through the slits in her dress. Instead, you look at the last spatter of rain caught in the city lights. Rivulets of water find each other and streak back, sliding down the glass like tears down cheeks.

You tell Lily to pull over by an all-night drugstore you know has a bank machine. You pull some cash out of your account. You don't need much for now, just enough to operate until you can get out of town. The machine's jaws open and two hundred dollars in crisp, new twenties slide out. You break a twenty and buy a bottle of painkillers and a couple of bottles of water. Back in the car, you knock back twice the recommended dose of pills and finish one of the water bottles in one go. You close your eyes and wait for the medicine to do its work, but before the throbbing eases, Lily swings the wheel and you're in the parking lot behind Pete's after-hours club. You first met Lily on the dance floor here on salsa night.

"Daddy wants to see you," she says.

If you had time to think this through, you never would have gone in to face Pete Vasquez. Lily's already out of the car. You follow her like a puppy dog.

You'd follow Lily across heaven and earth. And hell, too, as it turns out.

THE CIRCLE OF LIGHT

The line of Tuesday late-night partygoers stretches down the alley that leads to the side entrance to the club. They're mostly kids of the ungrateful living generation, ironically trying to keep Goth alive. Their clothes match their black eyeliner: *tons* of black eyeliner, drugstores and mothers' bathroom drawers full of black eyeliner. It's a parade of sad raccoons who don't have that much to complain about and they're pissed off about that, too.

The posers are interspersed with a few hardcore, outlandishly dressed party kids. They look like they all escaped from the same circus. The theme tonight appears to be Irish Vampire Clowns. They're beyond pale, dressed in bright green. They wear curly antennae on their heads that end with big cherry lollipops. It's like they're part of some kind of twisted sports team, if cutting were a sport. You're not much older than these kids. Not in chronological age, anyway.

The club, called *Como Si*, is in the basement. Officially, Pete owns the bodega on the main floor and the top floor houses his accounting business.

Pete's crew of two old guys and one old lady — Lily's grandmother — work the phones for his bookie operation upstairs. Pete doesn't get along so well with his mother, so he hangs out in the back of the bodega smoking and talking on his cell phone and admiring his black Caddy in the rear parking lot.

Pete only drives the Cadillac to make the rounds of a few laundromats he says he "has an interest in." Pete started out as an enforcer for The Machine and still picks up weekly payments, leaning on mom and pop businesses. "I came up when the Korean laundromat biz was exploding. Koreans don't call the cops. Protection's a beautiful thing. I swing in, maybe pick up or drop off some laundry and there's always a white envelope. It's like being a bill collector for the government. It doesn't even occur to them to give any flack."

Maybe that's because Pete's rep as a guy not to mess with lives on from the old days.

Lily's halfway to the back door and you're stumbling after her. Sitting in the passenger seat for the ride to *Como Si*, you've stiffened up and your body feels old. *Thank you, Denny.* Likely Denny's body is slowly sliding down some bloody rebar, so you really can't hold a grudge over a few aches and pains. You're only halfway across the back lot and you can already hear the thump of electronica from the building's basement.

Como Si is the perfect New York after-hours club if you know the schedule. The regulars are a cult that somehow know the drill without taking notes. Wednesdays, local kids with electric guitars squeeze on the tiny stage to try to bring back the hair band, though everything sounds like REO Speedwagon on bad acid. Thursday the club is closed for cleaning, but it's really poker night on the underground circuit. Friday is always gutless '80s music. Saturday nights at *Como Si* are supposed to be like a Saturday Night Fever disco — AKA gay guys' night. That always devolves into an ABBA marathon. Sunday, Dyke Night, features a lot of Justin Bieber early in the evening and Melissa Etheridge lyrics rapped over synth later on. Monday is Lady's Night: Cool jazz and hot blues for the first half of the evening followed by salsa till dawn.

If Lily had taken you to *Como Si* on any of those other nights, you could handle this meeting with Pete better. But Tuesday nights like this? A DJ spins house music until 3 a.m. and *Como Si*'s walls thump until dawn with industrial clash mixed with that ambient shit that's only tolerable to sweaty kids on MDMA.

The beat, even in the parking lot, matches your headache's pace. This ear beating makes you wish you were back in Havana by the Hudson. Salsa till dawn (every night) is your preference. Tia Marta taught you salsa and English to make you a more acceptable boy. Sometimes, when you're on the dance floor with Lily in your arms and lost in the music, you could almost forgive Tia Marta everything.

Instead of heading to the side door, Lily steams straight at a steel door by the bodega's loading dock. She rings a doorbell that's hidden above the door frame. She has to lift up on the tip toes of her high heels to do it and you watch her bare legs working, the long calf muscles contracting under taut skin. Lily teaches Zumba part-time at a nearby gym and it shows. Her exercise class was your in with Lily and how you found the courage to talk to her. Since she did Zumba, she thought she knew salsa. You showed her the difference between what she was doing and true salsa from Miami. Salsa is the only thing you and Lily both do that you execute better. You've got the looks and the clothes — at least you did until Denny's fist pounded your face sideways and flat — but, no salsa? No Lily.

The peephole darkens for a moment and you hear three heavy deadlocks ratchet and clunk. Jake Cibrian swings the door open and drinks your girl up and down slowly. "Hello, gorgeous." Jake has one of those too-wide, shark smiles that shows two rows of sharp teeth. "You looking to skip the line and do some thumpin'?" He's hard-muscle packed into a suit that doesn't fit him in the shoulders. The jacket hangs straight down like he bought a big polyester shopping bag off the rack.

Jake sees you step into the light behind Lily and his mouth forms a big zero through which a trilling, girlish giggle escapes. "If it ain't the little Cuban! Hey, Cube! Jesus Diaz, the Cuban sensation! The Cuban *burning* sensation. You get hit by a truck?"

"Cut myself shaving."

"Was you shaving with a machete?"

You would have come up with something cutting, but just then your nose starts to bleed again, defying the sheer force of your will. You cover it with your handkerchief and step in front of Lily.

"Never mind busting his balls, Jake. Busting his nut is my job."

Despite the pain in your jaw, you give Jake a smile. It hurts, but for the look on his mug, it feels better somehow, too.

"He's here to talk to my dad," Lily says.

"Pete's in back with his noise-cancelling headphones. You musta messed up real bad to get Pete out of bed, Cube. He's hardly ever here once *Como Si* opens. C'mon in."

He steps aside and you look back to make room for the lady, but Lily's already retreating to her car. She blows you a kiss. "Keep pressure on it, up near the bridge of your nose. Come see me after, if it's not too late." She's already floating away like a rose petal on the wind.

Your stuff is in the car and you're about to say she should wait, this won't take long. Then Jake yanks you inside by the collar. He shoves you back a few feet while he turns the deadlocks.

"You shouldn't put hands on me, Jake. I don't like it."

"Easy, Cube. Pete wants to see you now, not later. The longer he stays, the more pissed he gets. I like it, but he's too old for this music."

The wooden floor vibrates with the pumping bass line while something wafts up, muffling a chorus that sounds vaguely familiar. Madonna or Gaga? As you follow Jake down the hallway, you're almost sure the beat is banging over a song from *Annie*, trying to obliterate it with equal measures of decibels and irony. Jake pounds his fist twice on another metal door and opens it, pointing you in. When the door clangs behind you, the music is muffled. You're in the loading dock at the back of the bodega. The concrete floor cuts some of the thump from the banging beat from *Como Si*'s pit. Sound tiles do the rest.

Pete, wearing the big cans of noise-cancelling headphones on his ears, sits in a circle of white light, smoke in one hand, a Kindle in the other. He looks up, holds one finger up and you stand at ease. A trickle of blood is thinking about trailing down your face again but you snort it back and tough out the ugly iron taste in the back of your throat. Damn Denny. He sure gave you something to remember him by.

Pete stands and tucks the e-reader into an inside pocket of his brown leather jacket before removing the headphones. "Jake bought me these headphones last Christmas. Says I can wear them on the plane. I tell him, where am I gonna fly? I come here, a drive once in a while, I go back home, I come back here the next day. When am I going to use these big headphones? Wear them on a plane, they're gonna think I should be flying the plane, am I right?"

He seems to really wait for an answer so you shrug and nod.

"No! I'm not right. Sometimes I work late and these headphones? It's a beautiful thing. All those freaks downstairs can go deaf, I'm up here counting their parents' money. I don't go deaf, I win twice, am I right? Sure, I'm right."

You nod, but you're thinking of Panama Bob disappearing into the dark air, then visible again, sprawled in the lit street. You couldn't see it from your high perch, but you can see the spreading pool of bright red blood all too well in your mind's eye. Did some woman across the street scream, or is that your imagination, filling in holes? Maybe you were the screamer. You're never going out on a ledge again unless the building's on fire.

"Siddown, kid. You look like you been through the wringer."

"Yeah."

Pete vacates the folding chair and waves you to sit. "Jimmy's looking for you. Wants to talk."

"He coming?"

"Don't worry about that. You talk to me. I'll fill him in."

How much has Jimmy told Pete about the demise of Panama Bob? Does Pete already know? You don't want to insult him by spooning it out on a need-to-know basis, but you don't want to be stupid, either.

"You want a drink or something? Some wine? Or maybe something cold from downstairs? You let me know and Jake'll be right back with a seven and seven, rum and Coke, whatever you like."

"No thanks, Pete. I'm okay. When I have a drink, I like it without Jake's spit in it."

Pete smiles for the first time. He gestures for you to wait and disappears into the gloom. When he returns to the circle of light, he's got two more folding chairs. He opens each one and sits opposite you.

You eye the empty chair. "Jimmy's not coming, right?"

"Nah, nah. I got a special guest coming. Actually, that's something you can help me with. He'll be here any minute. Jake spotted the guy in the line outside and we were just waiting for you. When Lily called and said how beat up you were, I had an idea."

"Lily called you?"

"Yeah, while you were getting your stuff and clearing out of your apartment and whatnot. Looking at you, Jesus, I have to say — and I don't mean this unkindly — my Lily, she did not underestimate. Did *Bob* do this to you?"

"Big Denny."

"Really?"

"Big Denny."

"How many times you shoot him before he went down?"

"Didn't. Humpty Dumpty had a great fall."

"Holy shit, people are falling all over the place tonight. Maybe I should sit on the floor, huh? Could get dangerous in here."

"I think that's it for falls from high places for tonight, Pete."

He laughs. "You killed Big Denny without an iron? Respect. And all this time I been thinking you were a pussy. No offence, but I guess Lily's right about you."

"Oh?"

"Yeah. She said you weren't that big a pussy."

You watch him laugh and you think how much more you love Lily than she loves you. You can salsa your way into her heart. She'll love you because you'll always treat her the way a goddess deserves to be treated. The skim will help with that project immensely.

Pete's laughter winds down as he picks up your silence. "Good. Good. Hey, now. You know what I miss? The angles used to be shallower and easier. Used to be, you bet on a dog race, you had a decent chance you could win. Used to be, you want to *fix* a dog race, that was even easier. This one time, I'm at the track and I pay this guy, just another ham-and-egger. Pay this guy a hundred bucks and he clips all the dogs' nails, you know? On their paws? He clips 'em all short but the one dog I bet on. You clip a dog's nails, he doesn't run quite as fast as the dog with nails. I look back, I think that was the easiest money I ever made. Made thousands on that one dog race and was home in time to watch the soaps with the wife. The soaps, I don't miss, but that afternoon with my wife, first and only time I banged her three times in one afternoon. No disrespect to Lily's mother, but you and me are talking here. Money is more than just money. It's juice. Not even on our wedding night did I have it like that afternoon."

"I understand." You don't. He's talking like he already knows about Panama Bob's skim.

"You know what else I miss, Jesus? Phone booths. Where did all New York's phone booths go? The other day I saw a homeless guy and he's talking into his Bluetooth." Pete laughs. "A fucking Bluetooth! On a homeless guy!"

You laugh politely. It hurts your ribs.

"All these civilians are walking around and it's the Jetsons. Everybody's talking to somebody who isn't there. People come into the store up front and no matter what time of day it is, there's always some woman in there talking to her friend while she shops. The friend's prolly got a job, but with the Facebook and the thing…they're not really doing their job. It's crazy. We all got jobs we gotta do, am I right?"

"Of course," you venture.

"Of *course*, of course! So I know you did a tough job tonight. You were doing your job. You got beat up, but there's no shame in that. The opposite, right?"

"Yeah."

"Yeah? Yeah."

Something about his delivery feels rehearsed.

"You know what else was good about phone booths back in the day? You want to shoot a guy, you just follow him around. At some point, the guy's going to go into a phone booth. You come up close, pop him in the ear while he's calling his mistress or saying goodnight to his Mom and *bang*! He's down between the 'good' and the 'night.' Phone booths! No place to run. No extra drama when you do your job."

"A phone booth would have been helpful tonight. Couple of 'em." The headache's hammering harder. How does anyone know if they have a concussion? Maybe you've got one of those hairline fractures that kills skiers when they run into a tree or something without a helmet, like what happened to Liam Neeson's wife and Sonny Bono. Maybe blood is slowly filling up your brain pan right now and you should have just gone to the hospital instead of coming here. And wouldn't it be great if Pete could just shut up or maybe just shoot you so you could go to sleep and be done?

He looks you up and down. "Listen. Seeing as you're here and all messed up already, I got another job for you, but don't worry, all you gotta do is sit there. This is going to be strange, but I got an idea to shake up the deadbeat I got waiting outside. You in?"

"What have I got to do?"

"Nothin'. Just sit there and look beat up. You can do that easy."

"For the next few weeks, probably."

"Ha. Yeah. But listen, as the guy who is dating Lily, you're going to have to trust me like I'm trusting you with my daughter. When the guy comes in, I'm going to put on a show. I love the theater. You understand?"

"Sure."

"Put your hands behind your back, behind the chair so it looks like you're tied up." You hesitate a moment, but you put your hands behind your back while Pete opens up a cell from his pocket and says, "Jake, bring the guy to the dock." He mumbles into the phone, circling you and you're feeling sleepy. You're still thinking about your brain bleed when the hard plastic loops of the zip tie cinch up and cut into your wrists.

You sit straight up like an electric shock has shot up your spine. You're wide awake and about to protest but the flat look in Pete's eyes tells you it'll be better if you shut up.

"This is even easier than a phone booth, huh?" he says. He gives you a grin and all you can do now is wonder how such an ugly animal could produce the beautiful woman you love.

THE DOCK

A knuckly fist pounds on the heavy door twice. The music from the pit below blares a moment as the door swings in. Jake Cibrian shoves a squirrelly guy dressed in black toward the circle of light. He wears a silver chain that hangs from the hoop in his ear to the piercing on his lip. When dealing with a guy like Pete, this is a mistake so obvious, it's visible from orbit.

"Edward! So glad you could join us," Pete says. By his tone, he could be calling a puppy to come get a treat.

Edward looks back at Jake. "There's no need to be rough about this. I called you guys. I called you and you said we could work this out!"

Oh, boy. This isn't looking good for you or Edward. You pull at the zip ties. Useless. The sharp plastic edges cut into your wrists. Pete left you your gun in the small of your back, but what good does that do? Throwing yourself to the floor and shooting the bad guys from behind your back only works in movies. In real life, the effort might annoy Pete. Then he might have Jake drag you over to the loading dock door and crush your head.

Edward rushes to Pete, the reasonable, older guy. He doesn't know Pete. He only thinks he does. The kid pulls crumpled bills out of his pants. "Just like I said! There's $400 there!"

"And that would leave the remaining bill for your bets at...?" Pete still looks reasonable.

"About thirty-nine thousand dollars."

For an older guy, Pete's fast. Edward didn't see the bitch slap coming. It knocks him sideways. "Never say the word 'about' when you're talking about money, Edward. Money's serious. Now *siddown*. I want you to meet my friend, Jesus."

Edward touches his cheek and sits at the edge of the chair, as if he might try something stupid like popping up and running. Jake stands with his back to the door, arms crossed with one hand inside his jacket. You know Jake's already got his snub-nosed . 38 in his fist. Standing like that is an old bodyguard trick. He looks like a guy standing with his arms crossed and looking surly, but his hand is already wrapped around the gun so if Edward runs, he'll whip it out, looking like some kind of fast draw cowboy in a bad suit. That's what you'd do if you were standing there. Wouldn't it be great if Jimmy had sent Jake to kill Panama Bob? If he had, it'd be Jake tied up in this chair and you'd be standing there with a smug look on your face instead of a spreading bruise.

Pete sits in the last folding chair and watches Edward closely. "I'm going to ask you some questions, Ed. I know you will answer me honestly. While we talk, I want you to look at my friend's face here. Note the obvious pain that he is in. The busted nose and the puffiness. He's working on blowing up into major shiners on each eye, don't you think? Most guys, they get worked over, it's mostly one eye 'cuz a lot of guys just think with one fist. Wild haymakers, same fist every time, pounding away. Most guys fight like they masturbate, one hand pounding away, am I right?"

Jake's girlish giggle makes you want to gut him even more than usual.

"But Jesus, here, got worked over pretty professionally, don't you think? You got to respect the work. His wounds look...symmetrical."

"Who *is* this guy?" Edward says.

"This here is Jesus Diaz. He's dating my daughter."

"Is that why you beat him up?"

Pete guffaws. "You don't know my daughter, Edward. Lily, she does what she likes and I just nod and say, 'What can I do for you, sweetheart?' And she still gives me a hard time. Nah, if Jesus is man enough for Lily, I got no complaints."

"So — ?"

"I wasn't done talking, Edward," Pete warns. "This is listening time for you. I'll let you know when it's your turn. Just keep looking at his face."

Edward shuts his mouth and looks at you.

"I *like* Jesus. He's a nice kid. But he's here in this sad state because you and Jesus have something in common. You're dealing with big problems, big people. You're over your head and I don't think you understand that. Jesus doesn't know the forces that are coming together. We're talking continents sliding around. Molten magma erupting in your face. Constellations turning upside down. And here you sit, a small person. You know what you guys are? You're Job, like from the Bible. You're both sitting on top of a shit pile and you're thinking of complaining about it, but you complain to God, you know what happens? You piss Him off. Trust me. I was an altar boy. I know. Job said, God, you take everything away from me. You beat the living shit out of me and kill everything I love and leave me just on the edge of fuckin death! What are you doing to me?"

Edward looks at you and says nothing. He's looking very pale, like the blood's draining from him. You're probably looking pale, too, and not just from blood loss. Pete's speech is as much to you as it is for Edward's benefit.

"So Job's a whiner and you know what God says to him? He looks down at Job with his ass on a shit pile and he says, 'Who do you think you are, Job? Where were you when I made the stars and named them and fuck knows what else? I am God and you are nothing to me. I can make you or I can break you and what I require of you is faithfulness. Never mind anything else, God says. Be faithful. Do as you are fuckin told or I'll pull you apart, put you back together and pull you apart again just for shits and giggles because I am God and you are not.'"

Pete pulls out a fresh cigarette from his pack and lights up. Edward glances his way and Pete points the lit cigarette toward your face. Another warning for both of you: for him to look at you while Pete is talking and a reminder to you that you are helpless.

"My old priest grew up Baptist in Indiana before he converted to be a Roman Catholic. He tells it better," Pete says. "He says, 'Don't box with God! Your arms are too short! Don't play head games with

God! He made your head!' That's somethin', isn't it?"

Pete pauses for a thoughtful puff before continuing. "I usually say *Roman* Catholic. Romans ruled a long time. I like the idea that I'm part of something huge. Me? And Jake over there? We're Roman soldiers. We got an empire and if you think you're Spartacus or some shit? We'll crucify you and burn your body and you'll be a goddamn streetlight."

Edward does not sob aloud, but he's crying now. Pussy. A real man curls up and cries on his kitchen floor when no one is around to hear him. A real man cries in the shower.

"That's what the Romans used to do. They'd barbecue a couple thousand slaves alive on a stick and the fire would eat at their fat and they'd be human candles, lighting the roads. Which were also bad ass by the way. I read that the space shuttle was the size it was because the Roman roads were just so wide for a couple of carts to pass each other. I guess it had something to do with the width of the axles. All roads lead to Rome and all roads are based on Roman measurements. Somebody decided the railways should only be so wide and the space shuttle couldn't be bigger than what railway cars could carry, so they based their specs on some Roman guy who built a road a couple of thousand years ago on a goat path. Amazing, isn't it?"

Pause.

"Edward!"

He jumps.

"I asked you a question —"

"Yes! Yes, it's amazing!"

"Good. Now you know what that's all about?"

Edward shakes his head.

"College boy." Pete takes a long drag and when he speaks, the smoke puffs out with each syllable. Pete transforms into a dragon spewing white smoke. "God. The Romans. Their roads. The shuttle. The railway. It's all about *faithfulness*. Faithfulness is the root of how things work. We got a *system*."

Tears roll down Edwards cheeks.

"I take the time to tell you this because I don't know what they are teaching at that school you go to, but it seems you don't understand the system and your place in it. You bet on a basketball game and you win, I pay you. You lose that bet and you pay me. You string me along and give me some bullshit, I start boxing, Edward. You're just like my friend Jesus, here. You're a babe in the woods. You don't know your arms are too short."

Pause.

Pete arches his eyebrows, inviting Edward to speak.

"I understand."

"Good. So my question to you, Edward, is how did you get here this evening?"

"I drove."

"Uh-huh. What do you drive?"

"Toyota."

"Toyota. Toyota, what?"

"Echo."

"Ah, the little one. Makes sense. You're a kid. You got a gambling problem. You own it?"

"Yeah."

"Is it in good shape?"

"No. I'm the fourth owner, I think."

"Okay, but you can get some bucks for it. The thing I'm trying to instil in you, Edward, is that you roll in here with four hundred bucks on this big a debt, I think you've got the wrong idea about our relationship. One time a guy came to me and he had his kids' piggy banks. That guy understood the system. He understood our relationship, see? The guy with the piggy banks? Bad guy. Bad father. Bad husband. But a good risk. He squeezed everything he had to come up with more dough before he came to me. When I look at you, I see a kid who's never been hit. Never got a real education. Edward, you are a guy who owes me a lot of fuckin money and you act like you can work this out without inconveniencing yourself. That inconveniences me, Ed. I got a daughter with expensive tastes. Am I right, Jesus?"

It hurts your face, but you give him a smile.

"Huh. That's good. You didn't lose no teeth. A miracle is what that is, Jesus."

You brace for the punch you're sure is coming.

"Give me until morning and I'm sure I can come up with more money. I just need more time. I can get $2,500 maybe even $3,000 if you give me until morning. Mom cut me off, but I'll make sure she knows...about God and Job and stuff."

Pete laughs. "Good! And I can help you help your mom understand, too." Pete flicks the lit cigarette into Edward's face as he rises and kicks him hard in the chest. The kid gets knocked over backward in his chair and goes sprawling. You saw a guy get kicked like that in Basic once. The sergeant's boot heel drove so hard into the guy's chest that it messed up his heart's electrical system and stopped it. That recruit had to be shocked with a defibrillator. Unfortunately for Edward, he's still moving.

"He looks as pale as the vampire Edward from

those movies," Pete says. "And dressed all in black, you look even more white. Is that the look you were going for? I ask because I'm a people person. Some guys, it's only about the money, but I got into this business for the people. Does that look work with the little chickie-poos in the club? Do you use lines on them like you used on me? 'Next week. I promise, I'll love you tomorrow —' "

The kid drools and sobs, which as answers go, doesn't accomplish much. Pete stands over him. You're relieved he's not thinking about you for the moment.

"You said we'd work it out!" Edward screams.

"We are working it out. This is me working out." Pete picks up the folding chair, collapses it and raised it above his head before bringing it down on Edward's ass again and again. "You're a little boy in need of a spanking!"

Edward doesn't so much cry as bleats. You've never heard a person in pain do that before, but he really does sound like a lamb getting the shit beat out of it.

"Your mom is going to believe you, Ed! She's going to help you pay down a lot of cash!"

You'd think the sight of Pete beating on the boy with a folding chair would remind you of old-time wrestling. It doesn't. In fact, the horror of his helplessness freezes you. All you can think about is the pain in Edward's ass and the look on his face because Edward knows somewhere deep down that Pete isn't even half done. Pete's just getting started.

Edward's cries grow louder. Pete stops and you think maybe God does have mercy. Then God pulls the noise-cancelling headphones over his ears and steps on the fingers of Edward's left hand, one by one, with his heel.

Jake ambles over, reaches down and rips the chain from Edward's face. The lip and ear hoops come away with the flesh and blood. Edward's cry of anguish is unforgettable. You want Edward's torture and the terrible bleating to stop, sure, but when they're done with him, they'll start on you. The scared and scarred part of you hoping they'll keep wailing on him? That's bigger than the human being praying they'll soon finish. Even in terrible moments like this, you discover there's still room for self-loathing. If you survive, you really should think about finding a shrink.

Pete's kicks are slowing.

Edward stops bleating and, somehow, his silence is worse.

Pausing to stare your way, Jake licks Edward's blood from his knuckles and grins. "You're next, Cube!"

You know monsters. You grew up under the rule of sadists so you know that, for Jake, a beating isn't a means to an end. Pain and power is an end in itself.

You are next. Think of something. Quick.

THE PUNISHMENT

Jake drags the kid away. Pete lights his next cigarette as he turns back to you. Pete's smiling. He's more scary when he smiles.

"As the guy who's possibly going to be your son-in-law, Pete," you say, "I'd really appreciate you untying my hands."

Pete smiles wider. "Let's talk first. Tie a guy's hands behind his back and sit him in a chair and... well, it keeps you sharp, thinking about how I've got a burning cigarette and you're sitting with no way to cover your crotch."

You cross your legs.

Jake burbles his little girl laugh, his back against the door again, arms crossed, his fist wrapped around the butt of the .38 in his fancy cross-draw shoulder holster rig. Some guys even have holsters with springs in them for a faster draw, like this is Tombstone and every day they face another desperado.

It's time to take control before Pete's burning and beating you and Jake is dragging you out, rolled up in a rug from one of the offices upstairs.

"In the old days, they called enforcers like you 'leg breakers.' It was a bad strategy. You break a guy's leg, he'll respect, but how's he gonna run and get you your money? Later on, we called the guys who were most persuasive 'dentists.' You break a guy's leg, he's only got two and he's fucked up. Knock a tooth or two out and the guy's motivated to keep the rest of his smile."

You smile, showing your pearly whites. "Whose side you on, Pete?" You don't feel it, but you have to inject calm into this situation, feel him out. He knows something you don't, but you've got to introduce a little doubt and make Pete think it's him on the dumb end.

"Panama Bob's dead, so not much use being on his side," Pete says. "So I'm on Vincent's side. Always side with the big guy with the big guns. Respect. Faithfulness. Crucifixion. These are the things that build empires."

"There's more sides to this than just Vincent's."

The folding chair scrapes across the cement as Pete pulls it close and sits to stare in your eyes. On the one hand, he looks intrigued, but he's also close enough to reach out and burn your eye with that cigarette. He waggles his eyebrows and you start talking, unsure what the end of the sentence is going to be until you get there. You lay it out, going slow:

"Jimmy sent me to do a job with Denny." True, sort of. He gave you the job and you asked Denny to drive.

"Denny killed Panama Bob." A lie.

"I just drove the car and didn't know what the job was until Denny already did it." A lie.

"Jimmy said the hit was Vincent's order, just

before he went under for his surgery." This is what Jimmy told you, but you didn't believe it for a second.

Pete's right. Sitting here helpless does make you sharp. At least you thought so until Pete's first bitch slap rocks you sideways and your nose is gushing blood again. Pain is such a tiny word for the huge wave that crashes over you.

"I already talked to Jimmy, kid. *Jimmy* says Bob planned to take over The Machine. He had something big going on that he wasn't letting Vincent in on. Bob was making moves on his own and cutting the organization out. Jimmy didn't know what. Vincent didn't know what and Jimmy didn't want to let his father know what was going on until he'd confronted Bob. *You* were just supposed to bring Bob to Jimmy's house."

And there it is. Jimmy's got what the military calls plausible deniability and he's making *you* the goat. Edward may have bleated like a lamb when they beat him, but they'll have you making whatever sounds a goat makes in a moment.

"Jimmy Lima says there's a lot of money involved. Then you call up Bob's ex-wife to ask about the combination to the safe in his office. We don't know what happened with Big Denny. You and Denny are friends, Jesus. It's hard to imagine you killing him. Actually, it's hard to imagine you trying to kill him and being successful. Is he really dead, Jesus? Was it Bob who beat the piss out of you? If you come clean, I won't have to beat the shit out of you. Where's Denny and where's whatever was in the wall safe?"

When you catch your breath and the tide of pain in the bridge of your nose ebbs a bit, Pete's still waiting.

You decide to tell some truth and see if that works. "Jimmy sent me to kill Panama Bob. Jimmy wants to take over The Machine." Then you get an inspiration for an idea that could be the truth. "I called the ex-wife to try to get into the safe because I thought there might be evidence in there." That sounds plausible.

Pete stares. Maybe he's considering what you're saying. Who can tell what's going on behind Pete's eyes?

"You and Denny went about this all wrong. If it's supposed to look like a suicide, you don't hang around and rifle Bob's office. If it's a clean hit, you don't leave a body around. Murders? The police take murder seriously. Missing persons? Not so much. If Bob were a missing person instead of a murder victim, there'd be a lot less heat on us, stupid." He slaps you again, between the *stu* and the *-pid*.

When you open your eyes, he's still staring at you, waiting.

"Jimmy wouldn't have sent you to kill Panama Bob unless he'd already considered whether Bob was careless, a thief or a rat. You think the boss is an idiot?"

"*Ow*," you say. You want to say much more about the pain you're in, but that might encourage him to do it again. "Jimmy had already sent Cat to talk to Bob and Cat never came back. We don't know what happened to him. Jimmy and Cat are tight, you know that. Jimmy was through the talking phase. He wanted his half-brother dead. It was supposed to look like a suicide but it didn't go down that neatly... though Bob did fall down pretty neatly in the end."

"You're asking me to take the word of a tiny Cuban whose pretty new to The Machine. The one guy who could stick up for you, you say is dead. Are you sure you don't want to rethink your story and give Big Denny a call? How about I get out my cell phone and we get Denny back from the dead and he confirms your story."

"Denny wasn't so trustworthy. He was banging Jimmy's wife."

That gets Pete's attention. He looks like you slapped him. From the door, Jake bursts out with "Bullshit!" but Pete isn't so sure.

"*Sh!*" you tell Jake. "The adults are talking." You might have seen that in a movie once. As bad as things are, it still feels good to watch Jake turn red and go from simmer to boil.

"Jimmy's wife..." Pete is thinking. "They say the best predictor of future behavior is past behavior. Fuck! If there is anything I can't stand, it is faithlessness and ingratitude."

"Denny was trying to kill me when I pushed him down into a construction pit."

Jake leaves his post by the door, anxious to get in on the slapping action, though if Jake gets involved, it'll be punching and kicking. "You're saying Denny threw Panama Bob off a building and then Denny fell to his death, too? That's a lot of falling in one night, man."

You look Jake dead in the eye. "Shit happens. Life really is like a Coen brothers movie sometimes."

Pete slaps you a third time. If he slaps you again, it feels like no one will ever have to again. Your ears ring with bells that peel *pain, pain, pain.*

"What were you doing calling up Bob's ex? What was in the safe?"

When you bring your head up, you want to shake

it, but that seems unwise. Something might come loose. You need ice over your eyes and you need to stop the cut that's opened up over your left eyebrow. Pete really does just think with his right hand. He's not working you over as professionally as old Denny did. "Careful, Pete, you're going to make me asymmetrical."

Jake laughs that stupid, trilling giggle. With the headache you have, that sound drills into your skull and feels almost as bad as the slaps.

Mixing the truth and lies together isn't working so well. If Pete slaps you again, your head will spin around on your neck. You think about the pistol in the small of your back. It's still just as useless. Pete knows it's there, but he's not worried. That makes the pain worse. He knows about the switchblade in your sock, too, and he doesn't think enough of you to bother to take your weapons away. He respects you not at all. If you try to go for it, the best case scenario is you shoot yourself in the ass. Worse case, in the spine. Worst case, you shoot yourself in the spine and then Jake and Pete kick you until you bleed out. Yeah, that would get the goat sounds going really good.

Once you're out of the picture, there's no one to warn Vincent that it's Jimmy who's taking over The Machine. Jimmy who ordered the hit on his stepbrother because he thinks Bob killed Cat. The fact that you happened to kill Jimmy's wife's lover, too? Happy circumstances all around for Jimmy. Not so good for you in any way. Bob was Vincent's stepson too, of course, so there's no mercy in your future and enemies at ever turn. That's why Jimmy picked you, the relative newcomer and outsider for the job.

The fact that Bob was skimming from The Machine might even be a minor thing to Vincent. When Jimmy ordered the hit, you should have jumped the chain of command and gone to Vincent. The truth is, the moment Jimmy ordered you to kill Bob, you were screwed and from where you sit now, it's hard to imagine how you ever thought this would work out any other way. For Jimmy, this is about getting even for Cat's death, getting the power, getting the skim and blaming the whole mess on you.

Jimmy sold you out. Pete just wants the truth about the wall safe before he kills you. The truth will *not* set you free.

The arc of your life will go from Castro escapee to slave to soldier slave, to bag man to enforcer to a crime lord's goat. There'd been girls, but there'd only been one woman. Lily was your only port in this shit storm and she'll never know what happened to you. You're going to be a missing person. Soon she'll be doing the salsa with someone else. You'll just be another guy she knew for a time.

"What was in the safe, moron?" Jake Cibrian yells.

You ignore him and focus on Pete. "Future father-in-law. Remember when I asked whose side you're on?"

"Yeah. What are you telling me? That I should be on *your* side?"

"Nope. You should be on your side. When Vincent finds out Jimmy had Denny kill his own stepson, you don't want to be standing so close to Jimmy. Jimmy's poison. I just drove the car. I'm the innocent bystander in the struggle for power that started tonight."

Jake raises a hand to his forehead. "I'm going to need a roadmap. This trip is all twisty."

Pete ignores him and keeps his gaze on your eyes, looking for a flicker. "Vincent isn't going to kill his only surviving son, kid—"

"Which is one reason you should be listening to me, Pete. Vincent isn't going to kill his only surviving son, but he will erase the people under him. Jimmy's only as powerful as long as he's got lieutenants, like *you*. You should start thinking that I'm looking out for my future father-in-law. That maybe I came to warn you how things are going bad."

"Because you love me so much?"

You see it now. Pete has a tell. Just before he bitch slaps, he takes a slightly deeper breath and his jaw gets tight. His jaw is getting tight now.

"Because I love Lily so much. Something happens to you, she's not happy with me. Something happens to me, you're in the doghouse and Lily isn't the forgiving type, is she?"

That stops him. His jaw softens. "I think you're the only one getting erased, Jesus."

"Yeah," You roll your eyes. "Like Vincent rose to run The Machine because he's such a patient, understanding-type guy."

"Watch your mouth, kid."

"What if I am lying? What if you're right and Denny is still alive? Maybe he's out hiding the money we found in Bob's safe. Like you said, Denny is my best friend, but we both know he's not the sharpest. Maybe he runs with the money Bob skimmed or maybe he goes to Vincent to make himself a hero."

"If you believed either of those things, you wouldn't be here now. You'd be on the run with

Denny. You guys would be taking the skim and running back to Miami."

"Lily doesn't want to go to Miami, so you know I gotta stay. You know I love her. She's your daughter, Pete. You tell me how anybody could not love her."

"You're trying to make me go soft on you, Jesus, but I still got a raging hard-on here. Just tell me about the skim. Tell me why you really aren't on the run already. Did Denny want half? More than half?"

That's when you get a new idea. It's really an old idea. You heard about it from Denny. You drove around with Denny for hours dropping off drugs and picking up money. You and Denny spent so much time together, most of it with Denny doing the talking. He talked baseball and who was an asshole and who wasn't and he talked about what he read. All Denny ever read was weight loss cookbooks and books about the mob. Denny told you about the grift. It's how a Boston gangster set up a guy for a hit once.

"Where's the skim, Jesus?" Pete asks. Pete's jaw tightens again and he takes a deep breath before he slaps you. You try to roll with it, but you've been hit too many times tonight to be that fancy.

Pete hits you, not so much with the savage whip of the back of his hand this time. There's more meat in it as he drives the heel of his hand across your jaw. Pete really puts his shoulder into his work.

You've got one shot at the grift before Jake comes over and joins in. Then, whether you've told them anything true or not, it's all over and you will never hold Lily on the dance floor again.

THE GRIFT

A good grift depends on the greed of the mark. The believable lie is one that doesn't make you look too good. The best lie is in line with the worst people expect from you. If you say you did the worst thing the mark would do themselves, they want to believe.

"Look in my wallet, Pete."

Jake comes forward and opens your jacket slow, as if he expects you to be booby trapped with a rattlesnake.

"Not you, moron. This information is not for apes. It's for my future father-in-law."

Jake draws his fist back to punch you square in the face. It would have been agonizing beyond belief on a night when you'd set new records for pain, but Pete catches Jake's elbow.

"Take it easy, Jake. I can't have a civil conversation if he's unconscious from concussions. Haven't you noticed? He's had enough punishment and we're getting somewhere."

"You heard him, wage ape. Go over and guard the door. When Pete and I are done talking, maybe even an idiot like you will figure that you aren't guarding that door to keep me in. You're on that door to keep the devil out."

Jake looks at Pete, pleading with his eyes to scratch up his knuckles on your chin. Pete's eyes flick to the door and Jake steams off.

Pete reaches inside your jacket and pulls out your wallet. When he opens it, his face softens. There's a picture of you and Lily on Coney Island. Big Denny took that picture. Pink cotton candy made beards for your smiling faces. Denny took the pictures and went on the rides while you and Lily walked the boardwalk holding hands.

"I want to believe you, Jesus, but this is serious. This is not about you and my daughter. This is about Jimmy and Bob and the big boss and money."

"It's not about the picture, Pete. It is about the money. Look at the money."

He pulls out the fold of fresh, new twenties. They are so new, they look like they've been ironed. Real ballers in the mob do what gangsters in the movies do. In *Pulp Fiction* and *Goodfellas*, bills are always rolled up with an elastic around the wad. You're too neat to do that and you'd like to think you're too smart to act the way Hollywood movies say you should. You use a Calvin Klein wallet made of glove leather.

You might never have heard a chortle before now, but you're pretty sure that's it. Pete's gone from violent to amused. That is, until Pete says, "What is this shit? This is — " he counts it out, "$180. Are you seriously — ?"

"Pete," you begin to pitch the grift. "Look at me and look at you. Do you think I'm a dumb guy?"

"You're pretty jammed up to be called a smart guy,

don't you think?"

A swing and a miss...

"I'm sitting here and I'm out of lies. All I want to do is be with Lily and be safe."

"Where's the skim, Jesus? Are you trying to play me? Jake can't wait to take you apart and see what makes you work, you know."

Strike two...

"I'm out of options so all that's left is to tell you everything because you are so right. Anybody hits me again tonight, I'll swallow my fucking tongue and call on God to kill me."

Pete looks you over, still holding the bills, forgotten in his hand.

Ball.

"Take a real good look at those bills, Pete. If those aren't just about the best counterfeits you've ever seen in your life, stub your cigarette out on my balls right now and I won't even complain."

He guffaws. You went from a chortle to an actual, certified, fully legit guffaw. You definitely got a piece of that one, but it's still a foul ball. You aren't out of this yet.

Pete stares at the bills, one by one. His forehead makes three deep lines as he squints at each bill, holding them up to the light.

"You asked me why I'm not running already. Doesn't make sense that I'm not running already, does it? You're right. I'm not running because I'm going to have to take care of Lily soon. She's not going to live in a walk up in Queens over a deli, forever, *Dad*. Lily is meant to live on the Upper East Side and travel the world and go to those art museums she dreams of. Maybe our kids will grow up in a brownstone and we'll have a view of the Park. For that to work, I gotta stay and make big money. No trucks or heists or highjacking or shakedowns or running around like errand boys for Jimmy Lima. Bob wanted to make big money. *Literally, Dad.* Bob wasn't so smart that he could skim from The Machine and not slip up long before now. But he knew a guy from the joint who was an artist who gave him an idea."

"What guy?"

Uh, shovel faster boy!

"I dunno. Some tourist guy named Kit from Scotland, traveling through the US, got pinched on a bogus marijuana conviction. He and Bob talked in the yard and Kit gave him the idea."

Pete looks from the bills, to you, back to the bills. "You're saying these are *fake*?" He leans forward, studying your face. You hope the blood covers up any trace of a lie that's leaking out.

"It's amazing what they can do with scanners and printers, huh?"

You need a name. Who knows anything about computers? You spit out the first name that comes to mind.

"Freejack Jack figured out how to make it work."

"Freejack?" Jake says, incredulous. "The guy who lives in Jimmy's guest house?"

"He used to be a straight citizen college boy before Jimmy picked him out of the unemployment line."

Your feet are braced, your shoulders hunched. You're on a roll and talking fast, but if you don't hit this one out of the park, it's going to be a long night of cigarette burns and body blows and your pulped face will go through a sieve by the time Jake is done.

"Panama Bob talked to Freejack. Told him to work on the idea of scanning currency."

Pete looks at the bills again. The corners of his lips turn down. "These?" He rubs a twenty between his thumb and forefinger, testing the texture. "You're telling me *this* bill is a fake?"

"It really is amazing what they can do with graphics programs. They're even coming out with 3D printers now. You load up the back with plastic chips and out comes a Nike running shoe out the front. Currency is on the way out, anyway. By the time we're done, nobody will believe in money at all, anymore."

"Bullshit."

"Think about it a minute longer. You *already* can't pass a hundred-dollar bill anywhere. There isn't a grocery store from here to the West Coast that would let you give them a hundred-dollar bill, US cash money, no matter how real it looks. Try any store and they won't give you any change."

Pete leans back and you watch his face as he works it out.

Home run.

Now for the tricky part. How do you walk out of here?

"What was in the safe?"

"A few of these bills. Freejack's samples for Bob." Swallow some blood and stall.

Pete leans toward you, more interested than threatening now. "And the kid, Freejack. He's not working for Jimmy because...?"

"Jimmy wanted too much of a cut. I'm not saying it's wrong, but you know how Jimmy is."

You catch Pete's slight, involuntary nod at the

truth of that. Jimmy Lima is notoriously cheap in doling out cuts to employees. "Holy," Pete says. "Jimmy went to war with his own brother for a counterfeit scam."

You blink. Uh...why not? "It's a lot of money, Pete. Enough for all of us to have a view of the park. For generations."

"I don't buy it." Jake pipes up from his place at the door and ruins everything. Almost. "Hell, I don't even *get* it."

If you had to lay it out again, you'd screw it up and they'd change your name in the obit from Jesus Diaz to Cigarette Burned Balls. Fortunately, you do not screw it up because Pete comes to your rescue.

"You don't get it? What's not to get, dummy? Bob has Freejack Jack make fake bills, right under Jimmy's nose. Jimmy can't kill Freejack because he's the fuckin golden goose. Or the goose that laid the golden eggs or whatever. Bob tried to keep it all for himself and now Jimmy wants it all for himself."

Pete's turns in his chair, holding the bills up to the light to admire them. "Bobby...poor Panama Bobby should never have kept this from Vincent. That was a sin and ungrateful."

"Unfaithful," you say.

"Fuckin right!" Pete says. "Vincent takes in Bobby. Stepson, son, doesn't matter. Treats Jimmy and Bob the same. Then Bob sees this opportunity and wants to keep it for himself. Selfish. Selfish and unfaithful are the only words. I don't know how I'll be able to show my face at the funeral knowing this about him now. And Jimmy? Jimmy lies to me about Bobby skimming. Lies to me about the counterfeit money. I've known that kid since diapers. Knew Vincent since Sing Sing. And lies and betrayal is all we get."

"Where's the skim?" Jake asks.

"There *is* no skim!" Pete says. "The skim is counterfeit bills! Bobby was going to keep it all for himself! Jimmy was going to keep it all to himself! It's a disgrace!"

"All that was in the safe was these bills," you say. "Samples." You've switched from bleeding to sweating.

"This will kill Vincent," Pete says, his shoulders slumping.

"Only if he finds out what this is really all about," you say.

Pete's eyes come up and you can't tell what that look means. His jaw tightens but his breathing is shallow.

"Of course, the best thing for all concerned would be for Jimmy to get hit. Vincent would never have to know his own sons tried to screw us all over. Panama Bob's dead. If Jimmy goes away...it all looks like gangland stuff. Say it was the Italians or some other gang. It usually is."

"You're talking mutiny. You're talking about starting a war to save your skin," Jake says.

"I'm talking about ending a betrayal and stepping up and finally getting what we deserve. We do all the work. We should be rich, too. When Vincent passes — and how much longer can that be? —- *you're* the man running The Machine, Pete. Vincent's true legacy will be secure, despite his lousy sons."

Pete smiles and, for the first time, he doesn't look scary.

Home run.

THE SKIM

The official story Pete will tell Jimmy Lima is that he couldn't find you. Unofficially, he told you to go get cleaned up until he figures what the next move should be and when to make it. Pete tells Jake to drive you where you need to go and you accept on the condition that Jake doesn't say one word to you on the way. Where else can you go? You arrive at Lily's place.

When she buzzes you up, she's waiting for you in the hallway, her hair pulled back in a ponytail and wearing tight jeans and a peasant top. Lily looks great in Vera Wang and heels, of course, but you prefer her like this, barefoot and casually gorgeous. She runs to you as soon as she sees you at the top of the stairs. "Oh, my god! Jesus! You looked better before! Did *Jake* do this to you?"

"Yeah. Jake's an asshole." You smile to yourself. She thinks you're being brave, but really, you're relishing the thought that Jake will never have Lily now. Every guy in The Machine wants Lily, of course. You tell the guys she's your girl, though she won't call what you have with her exclusive.

"I have an idea," you said one day not long ago. "How about you roll up those posters of yours, marry me and we run away together?"

"They aren't posters. They're *prints. Starry Night* and the Dalis. And, no, not yet," she said. "I'm only twenty-three. Rush in like my parents' whole generation did? No thanks. That's stupid. Let's enjoy being young and see where it goes, okay?"

It was either agree or lose her. You agreed, but soon, with Panama Bob's skim and Jake and Pete chasing wild geese made of fake bills that aren't fake? Maybe Lily will teach Zumba in Miami all the way into her eighth month.

By the time a baby comes along, you and she will have set up and can play house on the same beach you washed up on so many years ago. Lily, pregnant with your child and playing in the sun and sand forever in back of a big house. That's a good dream.

She puts your left arm across her shoulders and tells you to lean on her on the walk down the hall. It's awkward and mostly unnecessary, but you lean on her anyway and put your face in her hair. Lavender. She bathes in it. Her shampoo is lavender. Her perfume is lavender. Every lavender candle and waft on a breeze outside a soap store will always carry a sense memory of Lily.

"I'm not here," you tell her.

"I'll make you some eggs," she says.

"You're going to cook something for me? Really?" Maybe you needed to get beaten up to ignite her maternal instincts. Nice to know she has some. Lily with maternal instincts is part of that misty dream of a life making sandcastles with your kids.

"I'm not hungry," you say.

"You need to eat."

"If Jimmy calls, you haven't heard from me."

"Eggs and toast make everybody feel better."

"Fine. Anyway, I'll have a nap and figure out what to do next but I'm not here, okay?"

"I got it, nowhere man."

She breaks off to let you enter her apartment door first. Your clothes are strewn across the floor and your go bag is dumped out on the coffee table. Given a second longer, you might have reacted, but someone pushes you hard from behind. You land softly on the couch. You look up to see one of Bob's lanky bodyguards with the tattoo of a letter *H* on his neck above the collar. His twin brother, Marv, has a tattoo very much like it on his neck. Same size and style, Marv's tattoo reads *M*.

"Hi, Harv."

"Hey, Jesus."

Lily shrugs. "Sorry Jesus. Harvey was insistent you get in the apartment right away. In case you were followed, he said."

Your eyes shift to Harv. "Jimmy want a report?"

"The boss is feeling hinky about the feds tapping his phones and his cell and his club and his car. Panama Bob's death has him way too edgy."

"So he doesn't want to meet."

"You tell me what goes, I go back and tell him in person tonight. Hey, Lily, can you make us some coffee, baby? Decaf for me, please, if you got it."

"Ain't your baby," Lily says, but she walks to the small kitchen just the same. Harv comes around the back of the sofa and kneels down. With his back to the kitchen and kneeling, Harv is a puppet show and all you see is his head and shoulders. He doesn't slap you, which is nice, but when he asks you where the key is, it's just as bad.

"What key?"

He sighs. "The key Bob always had around his neck."

"I imagine it's still around his neck or in an evidence bag down at the morgue."

"Don't shit a shitter, man."

"Easy, Harv. Sounds like you've got as much to tell me as I have to tell you."

Harv studies your eyes for a full minute before he speaks again. "You were in the army. I was in the army. Both a couple of grunts in this mess. Jimmy told Marv and me you'd be showing up at Bob's office and if we wanted to be on the right side when all this shakes out, we'd go see him as soon as you showed up."

"That's reassuring," you say. "Bob was convinced you guys were stupid, leaving your post just on my say-so."

He shrugs. "Marv and me, we're pretty worried. Jimmy's talking about telling Vincent another gang hit Bob. Last thing we need is a war with somebody just to throw blame off on them. Why can't everybody get along and make their money for Christ sakes?" Harv surveys your clothes strewn across the little living room. "Sorry about your clothes and stuff, man. I didn't take nothing. I just need that key fast. Nice suits."

"Thanks. What's the key all about, Harv?"

"Oh, man! You know it's about the skim. Enough money to get away from here. Enough for me and Marv and you, too, if you're smart about it. How about we pull the pin and get out before Jimmy's plan for world domination gets us jammed up? Marv talked Jimmy out of blaming the Italians, but he's still only thinking about covering himself. He decided to blame the Romanians! He'll tell Vincent the *Romanians* hit Bob."

"Why the Romanians?"

"The Italians are too big to wrestle."

"The Romanians are crazier. Smaller the mob, the more psycho they are."

Harv wipes sweat from his forehead and nods. "Valid. The Liberians have a block in Queens. One block, but they'd gut your whole family for squinting their way on a sunny day. Some Samoan kids? Midgets and punks really, but they got half a block in Washington Heights. They'd kill anybody over a rainy day."

"Seems these smaller gangs' moods are very weather-oriented."

"My point, smart ass, is, whoever Jimmy blames his brother's death on, it's war. Jimmy is only thinking of his own hide. What does he think Vincent's going to do about me and Marv? We were supposed to be watching over Bob when Bob got himself killed! Before this is done, me and Marv are done. The doctors are keeping the big boss in the hospital another couple of days. We gotta get out before the sky starts raining shit."

"I feel for you. And it sounds like your true calling is to be a weatherman."

Harv looks at you as if he just clued in that he's not talking to himself. "Hey, what happened to you, man? You look like a prize fighter."

"A prize fighter after his final fight. Denny rearranged my furniture."

"He try to stop you from doing Bob or something?"

"Nah. We had a disagreement. Keep it to yourself, but uh...Denny was doing Jimmy's wife."

"Christ! Him, too?"

"*What*?"

"Never mind. Jimmy's on enough of a rampage. He was pissed at Bob and wants the skim, sure. Jimmy wants Cat Fornes back, too. I told him, I don't think Cat's coming back and Jimmy got pretty hot at me. All he can talk about is Cat. You'd think a big, tough son of a bitch like Cat, jiu jitsu fighter, tattoos and all, could handle himself."

"Yeah, that is a mystery," you say, "but nobody's too big for bullets."

Harv looks away. "You got any cream, Lily? Marv doesn't let me have any cream. He's on a health kick. He wants me to be thinner. Every day, I look at him and think I could look like Marv and be more muscular, if lifting weights didn't bore the living shit out of me. Excuse my language, Lily. I got an allergy to the gym is all. Thin is okay without all the veins popping out. Marv's my funhouse mirror."

"Where is Marv?"

"Waiting for Denny. He hasn't shown up at his place yet. You weren't at your apartment, so I figured you'd be here." Harv looks over his shoulder, studying Lily's ass like he's cramming for an exam. "I sure would be here all the time if I were you."

"So the cops have the key," you say. "What was the key for? Safety deposit box?"

Harv shakes his head. "Storage locker."

Lily starts up the loud buzz saw in the stainless steel box she calls an espresso machine to grind beans and Harv looks back to study Lily's ass again while you bend a knee and reach for the switchblade in your sock.

"Where's the storage locker?"

"Dunno. Bob ditched us like once or twice a week. Said he didn't like all the babysitting all the time, but we figured he was sneaking off to make deposits."

"Then how do you know it's a storage locker?"

"We saw the key. You sure you don't have it?"

You're weary, but your switchblade opens at Harv's throat in such a casual move of your arm, he doesn't see it coming. "Where's the storage locker, Harv? Let's not let this get weird."

As the espresso machine's blades wind down, you hear the hammer of Harv's pistol click back. He's scared but he manages a smile.

You take the blade from his throat. You took a knife to a gun fight. Rookie mistake. You're going to have to talk your way out of this. You talked Pete out of killing you, but Harv was Bob's bodyguard. He knows too much. The counterfeit grift won't work on him. Or you could just give up the location of the key and Harv could kill you. That might be a mercy after all that's gone on tonight. But then he might hurt Lily. He'll kill Lily for witnessing your murder if he really plans to make a run for it.

You don't just retire from The Machine. You ask permission to retire and usually that's refused unless you're too old for the life. Harv's desperate and just wants to get the key, hit the storage locker and get out of town. He probably dreams of a beach in his future, too. A care-free beach is the American dream, as far away and unlikely as a lottery win.

"Harv, we need to talk about this. You have to think about what side you're on."

"What? You think I should be on your side? I be Batman and you be Superman and we team up? I never liked those comic books."

"No. It's not about that. Everybody's on his own side, but if you give me a minute, I can show you how pulling that trigger is not in your interest."

"I got a bead on you right through the back of this couch, man, so tell me where the fuckin key really is." His tone is scary because it's flat. You see fear in his eyes, but his voice is steady. He won't hesitate to pull the trigger. "Are we going to stay friendly or am — "

Kang!
Kang!
Harv's gun goes off, a crack that echoes off the walls. There's a new hole in the leather couch that's even with your heart. You *feel* the bullet whiz by, missing you by maybe an inch.

BONG!
Whiff!
BONG!
BONG!
Pete gave Lily fancy cookware when she moved out of the house. One of those gifts was a heavy iron skillet.

Lily's eyes are wide and she's breathing hard. Her pulse races in her neck. She drops the skillet with a clang into the pool of blood flooding from Harv's skull. She comes around the couch, listless as a zombie, and falls into your arms. Her tears are hot on your cheek.

"You did a good thing," you say, "especially since I had no idea what shit I was going to tell that fool."

Lily's breath is fast and shallow on your neck. Her

voice is muffled. "I *told* you you needed eggs. God! When do I ever cook for you? Take a hint next time! What happens now?"

"Which would you prefer? A life of riches on sunny beaches or to disappear into the country?"

"Do I get to be wealthy in the country, too? I can't be a hick."

"Yes, of course, you can be wealthy in the country, too."

"I want to go to Paris and I want to go to Spain. I want to see the Salvador Dali museum. I want to be anywhere but here now."

"Agreed. But first, I suggest you pack a bag quick and we have to do something about the corpse behind the couch."

"Solid thinking, Ace." But she doesn't move. She's still crying.

Lily dials her father and hands her cell to you. "Clean up, Aisle 3. The key's under the mat."

Pete says Jake is on his way back to take care of the spilled ketchup and the broken bottle, but you and Lily are already in her car driving away. You hang up on Pete without going into any more detail and turn it off. You tell Lily to slow down and drive the speed limit. After a couple of blocks and several urgent warnings — okay, pleading — that she's going to get you both pinched, she listens and eases up on the accelerator. After another few blocks, Lily speaks for the first time since she closed the door to her apartment. "Has everybody gone crazy? Harv... He was at Dad's barbecue last summer."

"The Machine's broken. It's already a civil war. Jimmy's going to make it bigger. Jimmy has his way? There's gonna be no crew left."

"Harv said it was all about Uncle Bob skimming."

"He did, huh? What else did he say?"

"He said he wasn't going to hurt you. He just needed to go through your stuff and ask you a few questions."

"You didn't believe him."

"Maybe I did. I wanted to believe. He was rude about it, though. I told Harv he shouldn't go through your stuff and he got very impolite about it. The way he talked to me...he talked to me like I didn't matter." Lily's upper lip curls. "When I got pissed about that, he softened up and apologized and asked me not to tell Dad. As if I'm a little girl who runs off to tattle to daddy. What a punk." She looks like an angry goddess. "Harv knows better now, doesn't he?" she says.

Lily really is like a goddess if it's true you're supposed to worship and love and fear deities in equal parts. You watch the streetlights flash by.

"So where's the money?" she says.

"I don't know exactly," you say.

"You better find out. I don't know anything much about civil war, but Dad made me watch *Gone With the Wind*. If that's civil war, I got an idea we should get out of town for a while."

"Absolutely!" But you don't know whether to feed her the same bullshit story about counterfeit bills you told Pete or to tell her you really are after Panama Bob's pirate treasure.

You decide to shut up and pray to God for help while she picks an out of the way hotel. You don't know which deity to fear more. God or the goddess? Looking at Lily, it feels like you are underwater, drowning again. You haven't felt trapped like this since...since when? Since the tire.

This is somehow worse than getting tied up and sitting in the chair at Pete's mercy. Lily's beside you, but you are so close to losing her. You close your eyes. You can't tell Lily the truth, so you pray silently, your head against the cool glass as the indifferent city flashes by. What can you tell her?

THE TIRE

The men who smuggled people weren't called coyotes back then, not in Cuba or Florida, anyway. It's only 90 miles of open water. America used to worry about nuclear missiles just off their coast, with Castro's finger on the button. Castro worried about Marines landing on his beaches. Your parents weren't political. They just wanted a better life for their sons. That, and there was the incident over the Montreal Expos baseball cap.

Marco Diaz worked as a bartender at the pool of a major hotel. Maritza was a maid at the same hotel. They met in May and married by the end of June. The ceremony was held in your father's childhood home in Pinar del Rio and Maritza gave birth to you eight months later. A couple of years later, you had a little brother. Rodolfo looked like you but thinner and more frail.

Your family was poor, but still better off than most. Your mother got the best tips. The tourists, especially the ones who returned year after year, were often generous. The newcomers left money behind at the end of their stay and wondered why the hotel help was surly. The seasoned travellers brought an extra bag filled with toothpaste, small toys and spare clothes and dealt out their goods for services on a daily basis. Those people, your father said, always left thinking how happy and cheerful all the people of Cuba were.

One day, an old French Canadian tourist arrived with a charter group. The man sat by the pool for most of his stay, slowly burning himself lobster red and ordering a steady supply of daiquiris. He wore a Montreal Expos baseball cap your father admired very much. Marco served the man well and spent much time engaging him in discussion about the Expos.

"I told the man how much you would love to own a cap like that," your father said. "I told him how our favorite pitcher was Nelson Santovenia. He was born just down the street from me in Pinar del Rio!"

For all his attentiveness and blatant hints, Marco went unrewarded. The day the man left for the airport, his Expos cap still on his head, your father came home, determined to go to America. "I *crawled*," Marco said. "What more could I have done? I wanted to get you that hat, Jesus!"

"It's okay, Papá. I don't need the hat. Don't be angry."

"I'm not angry at you, *mijo*. It's not even really about the hat. I'm angry at callousness. That man took advantage of me. I have a job, but still no respect. I fetch drinks for drunks. I've got no power or pride."

"We are servants," your mother said. "If we go to America, we can still be servants. This is our home. Different countries, same problems. Where's the pride in that?"

"It's only ninety miles away!" Marco thundered. "A better life where at least we have a chance. We'll have lots of friends there. So what if we're servants there? At least I could buy my sons baseball caps."

"The Expos don't play in Florida," you said. "They're in Canada."

Marco's laugh was a bark. He rubbed your short hair. "Montreal is too far to swim, even for men like us."

"Florida is too far to swim," Maritza said.

Your father found a man with a boat willing to ferry his family safely.

It wasn't safe. It was a dirty, old fishing trawler manned by the Captain, a strong-looking fellow with a stubbled chin, and his mate, an older fat man with a long gray beard. You shivered, surprised at how cold you could be on the water at night. You huddled with Rodolfo and your mother, trying to comfort your brother and warm him.

The boat's engine droned on through the night and, as the waves grew in height, the bow rose and fell. You and your brother vomited over the rail until there was nothing left in your stomachs. Next came the dry heaves. With each tortuous spasm, it felt like your scrotum might come up through your mouth. You can't remember how long you were on the boat. All you know is that you promised yourself that, after this trip, you would never set foot on a boat again.

You woke around dawn to a loud argument. You rose from the deck and saw land ahead. It didn't look far, but the Captain of the boat refused to take your family any closer.

"The weather slowed us too much. We spent more

fuel. The Coast Guard will spot us any moment. Give us more money if you want me to risk my boat!"

Your father refused.

"Fine," the Captain said.

You thought it was over. The man shrugged, his palms out, with a "What more can I do?" look, but a minute later he returned from the cabin with a rifle. Your father's back was turned. He was still staring at the Florida coastline, smiling, as the Captain swung the rifle's butt into his temple. He was knocked cold, a red gash gushed crimson blood down his neck and across his white shirt.

Maritza screamed but she did not run to her husband. Instead, she pulled you and Rodolpho to her and cried, burying her face in your shoulder. She begged for her family's lives. She had hidden a wad of American bills wrapped in a white handkerchief in her underwear. She reached under her skirt and threw it to the deck at the Captain's feet. The Captain laughed and handed the rifle to his mate.

Marco Diaz, helpless, moaned and grabbed at his head. The Captain and his mate swung your father overboard. Then the Captain held up the rifle and pointed over the side, toward land. "Jump!"

"The children can't swim to shore! It's too far! You're killing us!"

The Captain considered for a moment and his gaze flickered. He ordered the mate to cut the rope that held a truck tire to the side of the boat. As soon as the black tire hit the water, the Captain pointed again to the water.

Maritza shook her head.

He and the mate picked up your mother and threw her overboard. You grabbed Rodolpho's hand and pulled him over the side with you.

Rodolpho panicked and flailed. You had underestimated the strength terror can bring. He wrapped himself around you and you had to fight him off, kicking and pushing, trying to stop him from pulling you down, drowning you both. You had tried to save him, but then you wanted to kill him to save yourself.

When you began to choke, you tried to swallow the saltwater rather than drown. You thought you could but it was too much and you choked more. Your brother was killing you. Your father's pride was drowning you and your mother was helpless. The light in the water dimmed. Dark depths called up to you.

A strong hand thrust down and grabbed you under the chin and hauled you up to the air. Your father, his head still leaking blood with every heartbeat, had one hand on the truck tire. He pulled you and Rodolpho to it. Rodolpho sputtered and choked and held to the tire as tightly as he'd held to you. Maritza cried. Marco smiled at you, but one eyeball was rolled up so all you could see was the white of his right eye.

The fishing boat roared away. Your mother was still pleading for the boat to come back long after you couldn't hear the engine's drone.

"We have to kick," your father said. "We are going to make it to land. When we make it to land, everything...everything will be fine."

You kicked. Your little brother complained until your father slapped him. It was the first time he had ever raised a hand to Rodolpho. "*Mijo*, you kick so we swim this tire to shore, or we all die."

Your little brother shut up and kicked.

You remember the burn in your calves and thighs. The salt stung your eyes. The brine splashing down your throat made you vomit again. All you had was more salt water to throw up. Your arms and shoulders ached and your hands cramped in their death grip on the tire. Waves slapped your face and splashed water into your gasping mouth. You choked and sputtered and puked more brine in a torturous cycle. The land didn't seem to get closer or farther away. It hung in sight, mocking and full of bright potential you were sure you'd never see.

But you kicked. Little Rodolpho kicked. Your mother stopped crying and she kicked. Soon, your father could not. He slipped in and out of consciousness, at first for less than a moment. Draped over the tire, he dropped out of the waking world. He slept more and longer each time, losing the battle for light. Each moment he did not kick was another moment you were all losing to the ocean's waves.

The last time he awoke, he asked his wife how long he had been asleep. She didn't know.

She blamed him for getting all of you onto, and then into, the ocean. In the end, she blamed your father for being dead weight. You're sure of that. She didn't look at him. The care drained from her voice. Her eyes were fixed on the far away land. She did not turn her head to look at Marco. She only kicked.

"Boys," he said. "Take care of each other. Take care of your mother. And keep kicking. Always, keep kicking." He shrugged. His last words were, "*Se mire como se mire, te quiero.*" *However you look at it, I love you.*

Marco Diaz let go of the tire and slipped down and away.

Maritza Diaz said, "Don't look back. I told him we should have tried for Isla Mujeres."

You could hear your father struggle weakly, trying to swim or float, but he had too little strength left. You heard a few weak splashes and then only the welcoming ocean and the crash of the next wave over you as it tried to tear you away from the tire and swallow you as well. You imagined him dropping away, deep and below you, from light into darkness. Looking up with two eyes — one ruined, one keen and sharp — Marco Diaz would be looking up at you and your brother and Maritza through a thin cloud of the last of his blood.

In your memory, Marco Diaz has faded like an old photograph — there, yet not all there. You can still see him on the deck of the rusty fishing trawler, smiling at the beckoning coast, an oblivious, dreaming fool. The day he came home angry over his wounded pride is vivid. Your father held a beer but was too upset to drink it. He could only complain about the Canadian tourist. You see your father in that vignette as a broken man, bitter that he could not give you a baseball cap you didn't want.

In your clearest memory, you see Marco Diaz for the best of the man he was: You see his smile as he lets go of the tire.

And you see him in your nightmares: a one-eyed, white-eyed zombie, still searching for you on the sea floor, clawing and scuttling through the dark in warrens and labyrinths of cutting coral.

You gripped the tire, gritted your teeth and held your breath through relentless, crashing waves. You, your brother and your silent mother came shoulder to shoulder to push the tire to the beach. You did not swim toward America and the dream of a better life. You kicked harder and swam in terror, swimming away from that vision of your drowned, grasping father, somewhere below and behind you, watching in a solitary death...and *waiting*.

To die with those you love and to be responsible for their deaths is a horror beyond measure. A lonely death is bitter solace.

THE FUTURE

You wake up in a cheap little motel in Jersey and no one wants that. You don't remember falling asleep last night and this morning, Lily doesn't want to get out of bed. She's not hungry. She just wants to sleep. She's never killed anyone before, so she's feeling a tad sensitive about the whole episode with Harv. The fact that Lily saved your life by crushing his skull with an iron skillet doesn't appease her and when you make a zombie joke, it does not go over well.

You won't pine over Harv's untimely demise. The shower spray bothers you much more. Each water droplet feels like a stick pounding on a drum. Your nose is straight, thanks to your painful efforts in first aid, but it feels thick and both your eyes are black. You taste blood as you run your tongue over your teeth but none are loose.

Big Denny was a bulldozer in his day. "In his day." Like he wasn't alive as recently as yesterday. Your sense of time is screwed up. So much has happened since last night, it feels like everything is slowed down and you're noticing everything more.

One of your combat instructors was a hard rock

named Sgt. Devin, but of course, everyone called him The Devil. The Devil said something about focus and time once, how when the adrenaline is pumping, your eyes will dilate and you'll think you can actually see the bullets whizzing by. You go into bullet-time like in a video game and you focus on details.

"Don't focus on the wrong details," The Devil said. "The wrong details will get you killed." Is that what you are doing now? Jimmy Lima's on the warpath and he doesn't care who gets hurt as long as it's not him. Instead of sitting at the bottom of a motel shower in Jersey crying over Denny, you should be getting the money and grabbing Lily for a run back to Miami or even someplace boring as long as it's far away from here.

Focus on the storage locker, dumbass.

Reassess: You have to find Panama Bob's storage locker before anyone else opens it. Jimmy wants the skim. Pete thinks the skim is a load of counterfeit money and a ticket to becoming the Boss. Now is not the time to hit the pause button.

The shower and fresh clothes make you feel a little more human. You may never feel like your old self again, but Armani salves a lot of wounds. You tell Lily you'll be a while but you'll bring back coffee. You slip out the door and take a walk. Within five blocks you find an Internet cafe. You order a bagel with some lox and a medium roast Tanzanian Peaberry coffee. Even in an armpit off the Jersey turnpike, you can still order a fancy coffee.

Your Internet search reveals a couple of storage companies by the Brooklyn Bridge and another cluster north of the meatpacking district. The heat is soothing and the caffeine helps you focus, but your jaw is so sore, the bagel takes a lot of time to get down. Halfway through the bagel, you think you've found the most likely target.

Most of the storage facilities are the indoor type with lots of security. Bob would want a place close to his building, but easy to get in and out of without a lot of fuss. Bob never walked anywhere unless he had to, so it's hardly a surprise when you discover a storage business on Greene Street. It's less than two blocks from Panama Bob's office. It's not a converted office building like most storage places. Instead, from Google Maps, it looks like several rows of little garages across from a big Post Office. Bob's key looked like it would fit a padlock rather than a regular door.

Next all you have to do is grab the key from the bathroom at the pizza place, get to the storage locker and get out of the line of fire. "Easy-peasy, lemon squeezy," as Tia Marta used to say as she gave your balls a rough squeeze.

"I love American idioms," she'd say in her thick German accent. "They are so nonsensical. A fat chance and a thin chance is the same to them. They say across the street and *right* across the street and that means the same. Americans say a healthy helping of food but that looks very different from a healthy helping of food."

Tia Marta looked down on Americans, but she'd chosen to come here. She called you a dirty boy when she found you in the basement, but then she'd held you all night and let you cry into her shoulder when you told her about how your father died. She helped you, but hurt you, too. Americans weren't the only people full of contradictions. She made you love her...at first.

You're almost back to the motel with a BLT and a coffee for Lily when your phone rings. The caller ID says it's Pete. You let it ring through to voicemail as you search out a public telephone. Pete's right. Finding a phone is harder than it used to be and there are no phone booths.

At a strip plaza, you find a bank of three phones with the telephone books ripped to pieces and only one of the phones works. You wipe it off with your handkerchief before you put the receiver anywhere near your mouth. You remember Tia Marta saying that a gentleman always carries a handkerchief, which was ironic because she did not allow you any clothes. She was right, though. With a handkerchief you can blow your nose, bandage a wound, conceal your identity, gag or even strangle a guy if you have to.

You call Pete on his private phone, the one he's sure isn't bugged. He answers after one ring.

"Lily safe?"

"Yeah." After last night, it's nice to hear worry in Pete's voice. "She's freaked out and won't get out of bed, but that's natural."

"Oh God... Listen, don't go back to her apartment."

"Does Jimmy have somebody watching it?"

"Ah. Geez. I wasn't thinking about that possibility. No, Jake, the idiot, used way too much bleach. We'll have to air it out before it's safe. The moron put bleach on top of ammonia! By the time I showed up to see what he was up to, he was almost passing out on top of the...uh, ketchup."

"Tragic."

"Bleach and ammonia don't go together! Am I the

only one around here who knows anything? Christ!"

There are so many ways to die. Denny's dead yet Jake lives. There are so many ways for things to go ugly, so many ways to end up dead and disappointed.

"Too bad you found him. Jake could have been on one of those *Most Moronic Criminals* shows or *1,000 Ways to Die* or something."

"What did Harv tell you before he got his bottle broke?"

Pete assumes it was you who killed Harv. That's fine. "If he was telling the truth, we got a civil war within The Machine up one nostril and war with the Romanians up the other. Jimmy will do whatever he can to make Vincent think it wasn't him who ordered Bob's hit. But no matter what Jimmy says, the Romanians have nothing to do with it. This is an in-house matter and Jimmy's making things worse."

"If Jimmy blames the Romanians, then you're in the clear."

"I thought about that. It would be nice to be in the clear, but as soon as the police let Vincent know how the investigation is progressing, I'll be the slaughtered goat. Camera caught my face on the way out and witnesses in the street saw Denny. Maybe me, too, if somebody was looking out the window at the lightning storm. Either you move up in the ranks and save me from Jimmy and Vincent, or I'm dead."

You listen to Pete breathe and when he says nothing, you add, "Jimmy sent Harv over to Lily's apartment. With him dead, Jimmy might decide to clean house, including you and Lily. It's not mutiny when the officers are trying to kill their own soldiers, Pete. Your loyalty is to Vincent, not his asshole son who is too ambitious for anybody's good."

"Yeah," Pete says. "I get it. It's me or him. I should have known. Jimmy was an asshole even when he was a cute little kid."

"Is the old man awake? How'd his surgery go?"

"Of course. He'll be fine. Vincent can't be killed. He's bulletproof. He's fuckin' immortal. Vincent Lima took three bullets in the '80s on three separate occasions before he got to the top. You watch. They whipped out the guy's prostate" — he pronounces it *prostrate* — "through a smokin' hole. Give 'em a few weeks and a Viagra and he'll be down at the strip club talkin' a stripper out to his car with nothing but a smile and a bindle of coke."

You ask Pete if he's talked to Vincent yet.

"How am I supposed to tell him one son's dead by the other's hand and his heir apparent is going to get us all killed?"

You consider this and think about the seeds you planted last night when he had you tied up and was threatening to burn your balls with cigarettes. "There's the other way," you say.

"What are you saying, Jesus?"

"I'm saying Vincent needs a new heir apparent. A guy with a steady hand on The Machine's wheel. Somebody who goes back a long way with Vincent. You could do the right thing and kill Jimmy and never tell Vincent you did him a solid."

"You're talking mutiny and treachery and some evil Shakespearian shit there, Jesus."

"I'm talking about being faithful to Vincent's legacy. Jimmy's already stirring up trouble with the *Banda*. If Jimmy were to end up shot, it would follow that the Romanians got Bob and then they went after Jimmy."

The wrinkle for Pete is that there'd still be a bloody gang war. Not your problem. The heat would be off you long enough to disappear with Lily. The security cam won't be a problem with you a thousand miles away.

"The old man thinks his dumb ass *sons* are his legacy," Pete says.

"Man plans, God pulls down Man's pants and mocks. Vincent's legacy should be preserving The Machine, not grinding the gears and ripping out the works."

"What I've said before sarcastically, I now say in earnest. You're smart, Jesus. Look after my little girl while I sort this out. When I'm Vincent's Number Two, you're coming up in the world and we'll have a sweet project what with all that sweet fake dough and all."

Good. Let the wise guys chase each other around while you slip out of the way and down the I-95. You could go Down Under (mob-speak for Florida and your old stomping grounds.) They do have some useful gun laws down in Florida and you do miss the beach.

Orlando is a nice, relatively war-free zone. Mob clashes too close to Disney would alarm the tourists and bring down the Feds' wrath so organized crime steers clear. The Families, Companies, Corporations, Machines, Bands, Clubs, Tribes and Offices all leave Orlando alone so the profits go to the Mouse. Besides, even gangsters want to take their kids to Disney and not have to worry.

Maybe Florida is too obvious and Jimmy would come looking. There's that little town up in Maine along the coast you've heard about. Poeticule Bay. All they've got up there is a lighthouse, a tiny police department that hands out speeding tickets and a view of the seagulls to one side and a view of the woods on the other. It was in the papers when the town's sheriff went missing. The body was never found. If they can lose a cop, you can certainly go invisible ninja and disappear there. Poeticule Bay would still be close enough, you might even duck into the Big Apple to visit your tailor down in the Village.

But what are you going to tell Lily and will she come with you? When Pete rises to the top, he'll leave you alone as long as you're married to his daughter. Once things settle down, maybe you could come back to New York. You'll need a couple kids by then, just for extra insurance. Pete's tough, but he won't mess with the father of his grandchildren. At least, you don't think he will. A lot of this will depend on Lily. You'll give her whatever she wants if she'll just stay with you, anything at all for her smile.

You've already been away too long and it's not like your body has recovered from Denny's beating and getting slapped around by Pete. In fact, if anything, you're more sore now than you were this morning. You need to get the coffee into Lily, cheer her up and make her eat. Then you'll curl up next to her, sleep, recover and wait until dark to get back to the pizza place in Tribeca. You'll get the key.

Then it's on to the Greene Street storage locker to see what treasures Bob buried. It seems like the perfect plan, but there *are* so many ways to die. Even as you snuggle up, spooning Lily, feeling her warmth and the softness of the pillow at your cheek, you have an inkling. Things have not gone well for you in the last twenty-four hours. The worst should be behind you. It should be easy from here on out.

Then you think of what you told Pete last night. It was the one thing you said that was unadulterated truth: Sometimes life really is like a Coen brothers' movie. Coen brothers movies are your favorites: *The Big Lebowski, Fargo, O Brother Where Art Thou?, No Country for Old Men, The Man Who Wasn't There, Blood Simple* and *A Serious Man.* Their movies ring ludicrous and true because things keep going wrong on the wide and easy road out of town.

"What are you thinking about?" Lily asks.

Your face is in her hair and your nose must not be too bad because you can get a whiff of lavender. You can't tell her any of this. "I was just thinking about *Fargo.* Remember how it was raining and we bought it from the guy with the box of DVDs on the sidewalk down by the Chambers subway, after we went into that Jamba Juice that time?"

"Yes."

"Remember how neither of us had seen the movie and we didn't have any expectations? We didn't know a thing about that movie. It had slipped below our radar somehow so when we watched it, it was this big surprise because we expected so little and got so much. Wouldn't it be great if everything worked like that?"

"Are you saying I expect too much out of life?" Lily asks.

"No, no.... I'm just saying how great it is when things work out, like you go for normal and you get great."

"Do you think we'll ever get to normal after this?"

You're still talking into the back of her head.

"Wouldn't regular, old *normal* be great? We could live like regular people. Be one of those citizens you see all the time, running off to a job somewhere, paying taxes and having kids."

She rolls over and stares at your broken face, studying your black eyes. "You want to have a regular job and pay taxes?"

It still hurts to smile. "Well, maybe not that part. But something close to normal would be great. Great is great, but for people like us? After this? Just normal would be great, too, wouldn't it?"

"I guess so. When can we start with normal, Jesus? I mean, we're falling asleep in a cheap little motel in Jersey. No one wants that."

You laugh and tell her that's what you thought, too.

"I can't stop thinking about Harv. He was going to shoot you."

"He *did* shoot at me. He missed. Not by much."

Lily is quiet. When she finally speaks again, you can tell by her eyes that she's still back in the apartment murdering Harv. "I read once that they did this study about free will."

"Who's they?"

"They. Them. You know. People who study the brain and stuff. They did this study where they asked people to choose something. I don't know what, but they could see on some kind of brain scanner that the choice is made before people think it's made."

"What do you mean?"

"I mean the choices we make...maybe they aren't our choices. Maybe we're just puppets and there is no free will, like this is a play and God's just watching it for His amusement."

"So you didn't choose to hit Harv in the head to save me?"

"It's not that I didn't choose exactly. It's that I didn't really have a choice. Free will might just be an illusion. If it is, we're all innocent. I want to feel innocent. I'm asking, what's it all about? Do we really have free will or is everything predestined? Tonight, for the first time, I don't want independence. I want God to take the blame and leave me alone."

"Despite my name, this is too deep for me. You need to talk to a priest. I don't know about free will. All I got is...making choices? That's for other people. People with money get to make choices."

Lily lays her head on your chest. Her warm tears soak through your shirt. And you think of Panama Bob's skim. How much could it be? Enough to have choices, anyway.

"The worst is behind us," you assure her.

The worst *should* be behind you. Pete kills Jimmy. You pass go and do not go to jail, either. You get the skim and evaporate into the wind with the girl of your dreams. But the more you think, *the worst is behind me*, the more sure you are that you will trip headfirst into some deep Shakespearian shit.

Easy-peasy, lemon squeezy.

LIES & PIE

You find a place to park Lily's car near NYU and take your time, strolling and doubling back, winding through the city. You try to look casual, checking in reflections in store windows and scanning for any sign of a tail. It pays to be paranoid. You only have to screw up once and your head will end up on a pike.

There's a murder house in Jersey. Denny told you, though he was fuzzy on the details. He would only say that he'd been there once when he was inducted and it took two days for the tortured rat to die.

"I didn't have a hand in it," Denny was quick to point out. "I had to watch. Made me dirty. They got a couple of guys from out of town to do the work. They enjoyed it too much. One guy had a blowtorch. The other guy used vice grips."

That's the problem with The Machine. If Vincent has a place set aside just for the purpose of murdering rivals and traitors, he's wasting a lot of energy and operating on a bad business model. When you came back from Iraq and Afghanistan, you should have looked harder for work instead of letting Denny get you into Vincent's business. It looked like easy money at the time and the military had left you with a limited skill set.

You pass the Silver Center for Arts and Science. When you first got to New York City, dark from the sun, you did what every newcomer does and what no native New Yorker would ever do. You took bus tours with people from all over the world and stared up. Awful histories aren't just for poor people in the desert. Before the Silver Center was an arts and science building, it was the Brown Building. Before that, it was the Asch Building.

You remember because the name was ironic. Up there, 146 garment workers died in the infamous Triangle Shirtwaist Factory Fire, just over 100 years ago. Ninety years before 9/11, New York saw sixty-two people, most of them young seamstresses, leap to their death from a high building, some of them on fire as they fell. Just the thought of it makes you dizzy and you're out on the ledge with Bob again. You close your eyes and wait for the feeling to pass.

It was March in 1911 when all those people died screaming. Rusty fire escapes collapsed. Locked exits trapped young women in an inferno. That fire was a testament to the greed and unsafe labor conditions of the garment workers' workplace. The squares have their murder houses, too. You don't have to be a bad guy to get screwed over permanently by the boss.

It takes almost half an hour to get to the mom and pop pizza joint. You look around one more time and, sure no one's watching, you enter. The girl who was here last night (could it really be that it was only *last* night?) is nowhere in sight. Instead, a late middle-aged man with wispy white hair parted in the middle stands behind the cash register. You're halfway to the bathroom to retrieve the key when he stops you.

"Bathroom's for customers only."

"Sure. I could eat."

"What?"

Taking in the yellowed walls and the orange grease stains running down the proprietor's apron, you're not in the mood for pizza. The big pizza chains dress their kitchen workers in aprons that are the same color as orange pizza grease. Maybe this place is just as clean as anywhere else, or equally dirty, anyway. In a glass case behind the line of pizza slices — lukewarm for the flies under heat lamps — you spot pastries.

"You make that pie here?"

He shakes his head. The bakery next door supplies them. "It's why the small place is always better than the chains. We got the extras. You want apple or cherry?"

You order a slice of cherry pie and he tosses you a key to the bathroom. If you go south tomorrow, you'll be eating key lime pie in the Keys. If you head north...what kind of pie do they eat in Maine?

You unlock the bathroom door. You lean your weight against it to open it without touching the doorknob just as Jimmy Lima steams in.

You aren't obvious about it, but your hand is already in the front pocket of your trench coat wrapped around the SIG. You don't pull it out. You're pretty fussy about your clothes, but if you have to shoot through the pocket to wipe out Jimmy, you will. The skim will buy a lot more trench coats.

Jimmy puts up both hands, empty, and smiles. He nods slightly left and right. Two heavies stare in through the front windows. Juan and Twist each give slow nods and narrow their eyes, like they're daring you to draw in an old Western. Their hands are stuffed in their pockets, just like you, so maybe this is *High Noon*. Unlike that scenario, if Juan doesn't get you, Twist will. God writes a mean script.

In the movies, even the guys who are wounded pretty bad end up getting bullets pulled out by a mob doc or a veterinarian. In real life, if you're lucky, you get dumped outside an ER. In the unlikely event that you survive, you're handcuffed to a gurney and have to answer a lot of uncomfortable questions from steely-eyed detectives.

Not that you have any hope of getting dumped out of a car at the entrance to Bellevue tonight. Not with Jimmy coming at you. If you live, he'll call in a guy with a blowtorch and a guy with vice grips. Jimmy's the kind of guy who holds a grudge so hard he won't let you die for days.

Time to switch tactics quick: You show him your empty hands and surprise him by stepping forward and hugging him.

"What the fuck, Jesus?" he says. "Why haven't you called?"

And, now, ladies and gentlemen, the Academy Award for Best Performance Under Threat of Horrible Death goes to...

"What the fuck? What the fuck! What's going on? Did Pete find you Bob's stash or not?" You've watched Pacino do this in so many movies, you're sure you can carry this off as long as you sound angry instead of shit balls scared.

Jimmy's eyes narrow. "What are you talking about? Talk fast, Jesus."

"Did Pete find the fuckin' money?"

Jimmy glances at the guy dressed in the dirty white apron behind the counter. The guy's listening but he looks bored like he's practiced looking bored all day from an early age. He puts your slice of pie on the counter in a casual move. With just a little more oomph, he'd be tossing it at you. In Miami, the old Spanish waitresses smile and hold out the key lime pie on a saucer with two hands, like you're still a kid and they're playing *mamacita*, giving you a special after school treat. In New York City, the move is, "Take it or not. I don't give a fuck. Just eat if you're gonna and get the fuck outta here!"

New York. That's the attitude you have to make Jimmy believe. As in: *Take my word or not. I don't give a fuck. Just swallow my story if you're gonna and get the fuck out!*

"Gimme a slice of cherry," Jimmy says.

The guy behind the counter nods and cuts another slice. You take yours and head for the booth along the wall, but before you can cut the shooters' angles outside, Jimmy takes your elbow and guides you to a table in front of the window.

Shit. You might not just *say* shit, either. You really wanted to get the key, but you have to go to the bathroom, too. Like The Devil used to say in boot, "You will be challenged not only when you are at your best, but when you have a fever, when you are unready, unsteady, sleepy and when you have to take a gargantuan shit. Persevere, anyway, and no whining!"

Okay, but the heroes in the movies never got the piss beaten out of them, two big black eyes and a broken nose. Bruce Willis or Clint Eastwood or Al Pacino never had to con the bad guy, escape danger, save the girl, make an awesome getaway and at the same time desperately yearn to hit the can. The worst Harrison Ford ever got was frozen in carbonite or a scratch on his forehead as Indiana Jones. Boo-fucking-hoo.The guy from *24* never went to the bathroom though the show tracked every second of the day.

You glance at Juan on the other side of the window. Both his hands are in his pockets and his scruffy beard makes him look hard. Twist leans over and gives you a smile, but not a friendly one. Could these be the two guys who enjoy hobbies with blow torches and vice grips? Denny was always fuzzy on the details of the murder house incident.

"Can I get a large coffee, too, buddy?" you call to the proprietor.

He shrugs and tells you a fresh pot is brewing. When he asks you how you take it, you tell him black and hot.

Your gun hand is away from the guy at the window, but as you sit, Jimmy makes a great show of putting his hands on the table and spreading them out, lifting his chin in a jab that tells you to do the same. You put both hands on the sides of your plate and smile at Juan and Twist. "Won't the guys be cold, boss? We should invite them in."

"I don't think so, Jesus. They stay cold out there so things don't get too hot in here."

"What are you talking about? Hasn't Pete talked to you? I filled him in on everything last night." You lower your voice and lean in, "Obviously, you didn't want me calling you."

"Pete said he couldn't find you. Even had Lily out looking but no luck. I've been worried about you,

Jesus. I thought maybe you flew the coop with Bobby's skim."

You drop your jaw and then concentrate on looking more angry. "What? Fuck Pete! I went straight to him to report."

"Usually it's Denny who comes to the house to report."

"Usually Denny doesn't think on his own. Denny follows your orders, not Bob's. *Usually.*"

"Wait. Are you saying Denny tried to stop you from killing Bob?"

"How do you think I got this?" You wave at your face and dig into a big forkful of pie to slow down the conversation. You've got a lot of lies to keep straight.

"What happened? Break it down, step by step."

"I got Bob. I imagine you already know the details about that."

"Took the big dive, yeah."

You scan his face for any trace of regret at having his brother killed. There's still a difference between hard rocks like Jimmy and guys like you. His eyes hold no regret.

"I told the cops he was depressed," Jimmy says, "which might have worked except somebody in the street saw a well-dressed guy who looked remarkably like you out on the ledge with him before he went over. The detective tells me Bob's office was ransacked. When I gave you the job, did I not say to be discreet?"

"That was me on the ledge, yes. I chased him out there because Denny warned Bob I was coming. While I was in the outer office telling Harv and Marv to beat it, Denny betrayed us."

"You're claiming Denny warned Bob you were

coming?”

“I’m not claiming it. I’m saying he did it. Must’ve called him on the cell while I was getting rid of Marv and Harv. Then Denny showed up behind me as I snuck up to Bob’s office door. He was supposed to stay with the car and make sure Bob didn’t get past me and make a run for it in his Caddy.”

Jimmy seems satisfied and tells you to go on.

“Denny almost stopped me, but when Bob went out the window, I followed right after him to the ledge. Denny’s not that fast on his feet.”

Jimmy takes a small piece of cherry pie and dribbles some red juice down his chin. His eyes never leave yours. “You got the key?”

“I’m your hero. Bob handed it to me.”

“He just handed it to you?”

“He was bargaining.”

“And he lost that bargain. Uh-huh. I get it. What happened with Denny?”

“Screwed up. He was tearing the place apart looking for the safe, looking for money. I thought if he had anything incriminating, it’s probably in a safe deposit box. It would have been easier to find that information out if Bob hadn’t run out on the ledge first. I had been hoping to ask him some questions before we were one inch away from the drop of doom.”

“So you’re telling me Denny was searching Bob’s office and he let you back in the window with the key?”

“Naturally. If he wanted the key, he had to let me back in safely. We had to get out of there before the cops showed up. We couldn’t very well have it out there and then. If I remember my *Star Trek* properly, the Klingon proverb is, 'Only a fool fights in a burning house.' There wasn't a lot of time to dance, Jimmy."

"And later Denny blacked your eyes and made your face a balloon?"

Better to stick as close to the truth as possible. "No. The cops were already on the way, so he didn't have time to try to kill me for the key until he pulled into a construction site. He did all the hitting, but I got the last lick in."

"Uh-huh.... That's a good story, Jesus. So where's the key?"

"If Pete hasn't got it already, it's in that bathroom, sitting on top of a ceiling tile over the john closest to the door. I brought Denny here to try to hash it out. I needed to know why he warned Bob when I went after your brother...on your orders."

Jimmy's face darkens. A storm's coming.

"You gotta understand, Denny and I were good friends for a long time. I wanted to work it out between us. I was hoping he'd get his head on straight, maybe make that lapse go away."

Jimmy takes another bite of pie and chews angrily, giving you both time to think. You wonder, how much did the cops tell Jimmy about Bob's death? People saw Denny in the street retrieving the key from Bob's broken neck. He said they were tourists. Tourists talk to police. If it had been New Yorkers, you'd have a decent shot of them moving on before the heat arrived. You begin to sweat. You shouldn't have told Jimmy that Denny was upstairs with you. You tripped up.

The manager comes around the counter and sets the steaming coffee on the table. He drops the handwritten bill beside Jimmy.

"Pete didn't tell me any of this. He said he couldn't find you. You saying Pete isn't on my page?"

"That's not for me to say, boss," you reply. "All I know is that I told him everything last night at the bodega's loading dock over *Como Si* so he could tell you what happened. Sounds like Pete is trying to hang me out to dry."

Jimmy leaves the crust and finishes the cherry filling, chewing with his shark mouth open, grinding and mashing. When he swallows, Jimmy says, "That's not a bad story, Jesus, trying to put it all on Pete and Big Denny like that. Except, I happen to know it's not true. You're a good liar, though. You must be a good liar to have such a big supply. You must be Bullshit's East Coast distributor. I already got the key. We searched for it and found it twenty minutes ago. It was *you* who called Bob's ex about the safe, not Denny."

Shit. Forgot that. Maybe you're *aren't* the best bullshit artist ever.

And then it occurs to you. How did Jimmy know to find you here? The only person who knew you were coming here tonight was Lily.

SMART OR GOOD?

"Jesus. Now that you know that I know that you're fulla shit, you want to start again?"

"Who told you you'd find me here, Jimmy?"

"A little bird told me."

"I see."

"Did the bird tell you that Harv is dead? Or how he died?"

Jimmy's shark mouth drops open another fraction of an inch. You've hit him with news. "Harv's brother's been asking about him," he says.

"He came after me. Harv died...horribly, but relatively quick."

"When it's locked on you, Death never comes quick enough."

"You'll be happy to know Harv wanted to get Bob's skim and get the hell out of town, so I guess that's another traitor you won't have to worry about, though there will be plenty more. Remember *The Godfather*, Jimmy? You're Sonny Corleone all over again. The hotheaded son of the boss everyone loves. I love movies so much, I'm amazed I didn't spot the parallel before. Only you killed Michael. Well...

Panama Bob was no Michael. Pacino played Michael as a real smart guy. Still, Bob's dead and he's still got us running in circles for the skim, so maybe we all underestimated him."

"Don't talk to me about my brother, Jesus."

"You remember what happens to Sonny, right? A lot of machine gun bullets."

Jimmy's turning red. Good. It sure looks like Lily's betrayed you. What's to live for? Maybe if you get Jimmy mad enough, he'll do you a favor and nod to one of his mooks and they'll open up right through the window and kill you relatively quick, too, in the stereotypical hail of bullets. With the civil war coming, it's bound to happen, anyway, right?

"You know what other movies I like?" you ask. "*Star Wars*."

"What?"

"Especially the first one where we first meet Han Solo in the crazy space bar."

"Chalmun's Cantina, also known as the Mos Eisley Cantina," Jimmy corrects you. You blink. He smiles for the first time. "I'm older than you, kid. I saw it in the theatre first and own every incarnation up to Blu-ray. I've seen the first trilogy over and over."

"So you know the controversy about whether Han shot first?"

Jimmy Lima takes a deep breath. "Heh. You think I'm Sonny Corleone. I think you're Greedo. You're the alien guy with the weird face that Jabba the Hutt sends to get Han Solo — "

"But Greedo just wants the money Han owes Jabba," you add. "I always thought calling the bad guy alien Greedo was a little too on the nose, didn't you? Greedo? Greedy?"

"In Mr. Lucas's defence, asshole, it's a kid's movie."

You shrug and nod. "So who shot first?"

"Han Solo shot first in the original." Jimmy's leaning in, looking at your hot coffee. "That's what I saw in the movie theater. Later, Lucas changed it so it looked like Greedo fired first."

You nod. "In the 1997 incarnation, yeah. Lucas wanted to make it clear to the kids that Han was the good guy. But in real life, if you don't make the first move and shoot your enemies before they shoot you, you end up a dead sucker. Better to teach kids to be smart. Good is easy. Smart is hard."

Jimmy clenches and unclenches his hands, getting ready for action. "But they shot at each other under a table meant for cocktails. How could Greedo miss? It's dumb. Han shot first. Had to, if he didn't want his balls shot off. Shooting first is always the smart thing to do."

Jimmy Lima's eyes are fixed on the coffee cup. He braces, telegraphing his move a second before he goes for the large paper cup, grabs it and tries to toss the steaming coffee in your face, just like you did to Denny.

Jimmy would have burned you badly, too, except you've already ducked and deked right to step beside Jimmy, putting his body between you and the guns outside. You jab the business end of your fork into Jimmy's exposed neck and run. It doesn't go in far. In the movies, you'd snag the jugular or the carotid and Jimmy would be a jigging, pumping fountain of blood. Instead, you get a band of muscle and open his skin up pretty well. Either way, he's screaming and you're running.

You jump the counter and you're already running past an open pizza oven, past the manager and out the rear fire door as Juan and Twist focus on Jimmy. You hope. You don't dare glance back in case one of Jimmy's boys is lining up his shot.

As you hit the door, a high-pitched alarm goes off that pierces your eardrums and shakes your nerves. It spurs you to try to sprint harder. You can run hard or long, but no one can do both. You run until you're out of breath and leaning on a wall in an alley. It would be easier to breathe and you could run much farther if your nose wasn't a solid hunk of pain. Running makes your face throb.

Jimmy's got the key, but there's good news, too. Maybe Lily didn't betray you. Jimmy went for that coffee cup so quick and easy, like he knew that's how you got a fighting chance over Big Denny De Molina.

Denny is still alive and talking. Big Denny, you're almost sure, is Jimmy's "little bird" instead of the lovely Lily. Lily loves you, or at least she didn't rat you out. That's a start!

That moment's pause almost finishes you. You hear a boom and cement from the wall you're leaning on chunks out to fall at your feet. Another boom and this time you hear the bullet whine by, smack and ricochet. You look back, expecting one of Jimmy's hired guns. Instead, it's the manager with the bad haircut.

He's got a huge silver revolver in his mitt. He might have got you, but his hand is shaking so badly, you can almost see the electric current of fear jangling through him. He steadies the hand cannon — a Dirty Harry .44 — and spreads his feet wide and drops into a two-handed shooting stance. He'd definitely have blown you away with his next shot, but he's breathing hard and trying to hold his breath and thinking too long about sending you to hell.

You pull your gun and point it at his head. You feel the energetic connection between your muzzle and the middle of the man's forehead. Pull the trigger now and he'll have a small red hole in front and a sick, yawning maw of brains squirting out the back. The pink mist will be followed by gray and white and red: All the colors of a head shot.

The shakes take over the pizza man's body. Hunters call it buck fever when they have a stag lined up in their scope but can't stop the tremors. He sees your steady eyes.

As gently as you can, you say, "You ain't Batman."

The pizza man understands now that he's not a killer. He's a worker ant who manages a little place that sells bad food. You are the hit man. He lowers the revolver and, still trembling, drops it to the sidewalk. He raises his empty hands, shaking so bad it looks like he's waving goodbye. A tear rolls down a cheek. He closes his eyes and begins a Hail Mary as he waits for you to throw him into whirling red blades.

You should shoot, but he's just a civilian. You've done a lot of things, but you don't shoot civilians. There's enough war without bringing civvies into it.

You're off down the alley, running again. You run with your chest thrown out, your head tilted back, opening your throat to your lungs to suck in as much air as you can gasp, driving your legs hard, long gone and far away before the pizza man is done his prayer.

THE BUG MAN OF SURFSIDE BEACH

"Balseros! Balseros!"

You don't remember the last 200 feet to the shore. You remember the waves pushing you away from America's promises and back toward Cuba. Your mother gasps and curses your father. Your brother whimpers and kicks as hard as he can, which isn't hard at all.

Sometimes, maybe once or twice a year, you wake from this same nightmare. Sometimes the nightmare keeps going and you can't wake up. You relive the moment the Captain threw your family overboard and Rodolpho panics again. This time he succeeds in drowning you.

Usually, the part that wakes you with a start and in a sweat is you, close to shore but still no sand under your feet. Your thighs burn. Your calves cramp. The ocean floor rises under you, but not fast enough. Somewhere behind you, your one-eyed, white-eyed zombie father is still reaching up, grabbing, pulling you back, pulling you under.

The safety of the beach is close, but as you and your brother and mother kick and kick and kick, pushing the old truck tire, you're sure it's just a tease and a cruel trick. As soon as your foot touches sand, your dead, drowned ghoul of a father — a moray eel where his tongue should be — will rip you away from the air and yank you down into the dark with him.

"Balseros! Balseros!" someone yells from the shore. A cluster of people gather and point your way. Are they pointing at you or are they pointing at a shark fin rising out of the water behind you? Maybe a shark will get you before your dead father can. Either way, at least you will rest. You've got no energy left to kick. Instead of pointing, they should be swimming out to you and helping.

Then you remember something your father said about feet. What was it? It was important. Wet foot. Dry foot. You have to get to the shore and then you'll be safe. No one will punish you and send you back to Cuba if you can get to the shore on your own. Your father told a terrible story of the US Coast Guard drowning Cubans who were trying to get to safety.

"White men, privileged to be Americans by accident of birth, might use water cannons on us. *Us!* People who just want to have a better life! They would kill us for having the temerity to grasp for what they were given for free and take for granted!"

Your mother said attacks by the Coast Guard rarely happened, or might even be Castro's propaganda, but Marco was firm. Until you step on dry land in Florida with your legs under you, you're a slave. Stand up, and you won't be any man's slave ever again.

"Wet foot? We get sent back to Cuba," he said. "Dry foot? We go see spring training."

The baseball, you admit, could be fun, but you're

not quite twelve and all you can think about is men with water cannons shooting you far out into the ocean to die.

A man in a boat is coming. It is a fancy, fast boat like you've never seen. It is loud and painted white. A small American flag flutters behind the driver from a red and white stick that looks like a candy cane. You have heard of go-fast boats, but this is a rich man's boat made for racing. It is mostly made of throaty engines. Go-fast boats from Cuba could hold ten or more people, but this long, low-slung cigarette boat swings in front of you, between your family and the shore, and the engines seem to roar even as they idle. The man is tan, but his low-riding Bermuda shorts reveal bright white skin. Big mirrored sunglasses make him look like a bug.

You thought you'd drown. Or your father's hand would wrap around your ankle or that you'd die of exhaustion or that sharks would rip you in two and eat you and your mother and brother. Then you were sure the Bug Man was going to kill you with his monster boat. The wake rolls over you and you spit saltwater. Rodolpho cries out weakly and the wash nearly pulls him from the tire. Somehow, you and your mother hold on to your brother.

"Help!" your mother cries.

The Bug Man smiles and twirls his wheel. Far off voices shout from the safety of the sand, but you can't see land anymore. There are no buildings rising up to give you hope of rest and shelter as soon as your feet are dry. The Bug Man stretches out his hand and hauls you up first. Spent, you collapse to the deck gasping.

"Landed a fish," the tanned man says.

You thank him and beg him to save Rodolpho and your mother. He hesitates and pulls down his glasses to look you up and down. He smiles and turns to haul up Rodolpho. He's not ten yet. "Scrawny fish."

Your mother is spent, but she swims over with the last of her energy in an awkward, one-handed stroke since she doesn't dare let go of the tire. She reaches up, smiling at the Bug Man, one hand still on her makeshift life preserver. The Bug Man is still smiling as he reaches down to touch Maritza's fingertips. He then straightens and waggles his fingers goodbye. He turns back to the wheel. Your mother's screams are swallowed as he guns the engine.

You try to stop the Bug Man from taking you away from your mother, pulling at his elbow. You plead. You bite the meat of his upper arm.

The Bug Man elbows you in the forehead and you are dazed but somehow grab a rail and keep your feet. You go back to bite him. You were in an after-school fight once. A bigger, older boy got you in a headlock and hit your head with his knuckles. He laughed until you wriggled out a little and bit him on the back of his arm. He screamed in pain. Then he screamed you were a girl for fighting that way, but that ended the fight. You go for the same spot and the Bug Man yelps, too, but he shakes you off and backhands you to the deck. As your head hits the rail, you turn to see your beautiful, terrified mother, her mouth making a huge "O".

As the Bug Man drives you away from your mother, you do the only thing that's left to do. You pull Rodolpho to his feet. His legs are wobbly, but for what you need to do, he doesn't have to walk. He only needs to fly past the sharp and savage propellers whirling and cutting the water behind the boat.

The engines roar louder. The bow rises high as the props dig in and churn. The boat jets forward, throwing you and Rodolpho back against the rail. The shift in inertia helps you throw your little brother away from the clutches of the Bug Man, but not quite enough.

You're about to jump, too. You hesitate only a second or two, preparing yourself to follow Rodolpho into the darkness. That's just enough time for the Bug Man to bring a fist down on the top of your head, all his weight behind the blow. It's much worse than knuckles. It makes your knees bend and you can't straighten them. You are the nail to the Bug Man's hammer.

Dazed, you see the sun come out from behind gray clouds. It's going to be a beautiful day somewhere else not far away.

"You let my scrawny fish get away!" the Bug Man says. He hammers you again and bright day drains to night.

You stand by Lily's car parked next to the NYU campus, bent over and gasping for breath, waiting for your heart to slow. A civilian just tried to kill you. Bob's dead. The cops have your picture from Panama Bob's murder scene by now. Big Denny is alive — you're almost sure. If you're right, Denny's talking to Jimmy Lima and the boss has the key to the skim. If Jimmy's listening to Denny, Pete's going to jam himself up, too. Harv is dead by Lily's hand.

Lily. The woman of your dreams, the one who balances out all the nightmares, is waiting for you in New Jersey. She's waiting for you to save her from a murder rap and this life of blood.

You are Maritza abandoned in the water, screaming and unheard. You're watching the life you could have had slip away.

You are a helpless boy, denied victory and trying to do the next best thing.

Worse: All this? You're doing it again. Loss is the loop of your life. You've fallen into the propeller blades.

TOOLS OF THE TRADE

Big Denny De Molina's flop is Apartment C in a building in Washington Heights. The C is a real problem because, as Brad Pitt mentions in *Fight Club,* lettered doors are for sad basement apartments. You can't look in a window or check to see if the lights are on. You're going into the situation blind, but you've got to get into Denny's apartment. He's got hardware you'll need stashed in there. It's even possible that Denny survived his fall into the construction pit and he's in there, covered in bandages and waiting for you to show up so he can kneecap you and demand a sincere apology before he puts a hole in your head. Or Marv is in there, waiting to take you to Jimmy Lima and a very uncomfortable death.

There's no doorman or security. There used to be two secure doors to the street, but even the residents stopped blaming the slum lord after the locks were destroyed every time they were replaced. Poor people robbing poor people isn't just illogical, it's downright stupid. If you're well off and a junkie wants to run off with your TV to fund a fix, you'll have the fun of picking out a new TV at Best Buy that afternoon. When all you've got is a dirty mattress on the floor and a coffeemaker, you'll blast whoever comes through the door with .oo buckshot to keep your coffeemaker.

You've been to Denny's plenty of times, but never with such trepidation. You're operating off a hunch based on Jimmy trying the same scalding coffee move that saved you from Denny. However, you have to trust your instincts and the alarm bells in your head are going off.

Years ago, every door in this building had a gold-plated door knocker. When those were stolen, silver knockers replaced them. Now there are no door knockers. Now it's all colorful spray painted tagger designs and wary eyes peering from peepholes.

You slip down the stairs and a couple of black kids, a boy and a girl of about seventeen, walk past you. They barely notice you. The cliche is true: They only have eyes for each other. You take a moment to watch them go.

Lily is just the right height so, when you walk side by side, your arm across her shoulders, you both move as one person. She's your perfect fit. You don't believe in soul mates, but Lily is so powerful you *want* to believe. You're ashamed you ever suspected for a moment that Lily would rat you out to Jimmy. You look at her the same way that young kid looked at his girl. One day soon, once you have Bob's skim and you can get away from all this, you could be your true self. When Lily sees the real you — not the enforcer — she'll see you the same way you see her. You're almost sure.

You don't know who your real self will be, but

you're excited to find out. Getting away with no money worries or responsibilities? That's why everyone plays the lottery. That kind of freedom makes you a kid and you can finally have that childhood you missed out on. The way you grew up, the real Jesus Diaz never had a chance. You and Lily can find out who you really are together and you're almost sure that's going to be great.

Bare bulbs hang like dead men above dim yellow pools of light down the basement hallway. You wait at the bottom of the stairs for five...ten...fifteen minutes. Somewhere above you, maybe on a landing far up the old iron staircase, a woman is screeching. You only hear one side of the fight, so it's like you're listening to a hysterical woman screaming into a phone. "It's mine! That's all mine! No, no, you are *not* taking that with you! *That's* mine, too!"

Christ, man, just go. Don't stay to haggle over an iPod full of James Brown, pirated ironic Manilow albums and LMFAO. If all the sinners in hell screamed out their torment in one voice, this woman would be their spokesperson.

Tia Marta is in your head again: Ugly threats, jibes and bullying. You push those thoughts away, but she's never far. If you could fix it so thoughts of Tia Marta would never return, if you could erase her with a well-aimed, sharp stick in the brain without anaesthetic, you would.

You wait and listen for any sounds of life down the hallway. Harv said Jimmy sent Marv to stake out Denny's place. A new thought: Maybe Marv is in the apartment, standing over Denny's corpse and he's the assassin waiting for you to come through the door. If Denny told Jimmy Lima everything, Jimmy might thank him and then whack him so his plans for The Machine would be safe from Vincent. Fathers and sons, bosses and underbosses: All had secrets from each other and would go to great lengths to keep them secret.

Or maybe it's simpler than all that and Denny and Marv are just playing a quiet game of poker, their weapons ready for you to poke your stupid face in so they can shoot off your big, puffy nose.

You move up and unscrew the lightbulbs as you go. Only the dim light cast down the hall from the stairwell reaches after you with thin yellow fingers. You stop at the door before Denny's apartment. The door reads: *Mechanical.* Old pipes gulp and gurgle and some kind of equipment hums unevenly, like something needs a tune up. Denny often complained that he had the worst apartment in the building because of that hum. The sporadic hammer and bang of water in the pipes kept him awake nights. Sometimes it was so bad, Denny left the TV on with the volume way up just to mask the noise from the mechanical room.

If you had the job of knocking somebody off in this situation, you'd be a smart ninja. You'd pick the lock to the mechanical room and wait in there. As soon as you heard anybody messing with Denny's door, you'd pop out and blast him. That would be a smart ninja way to solve this equation, given the variables.

You don't want somebody popping out of that door behind you. You listen before you make your move. You can't hear anybody breathing behind the door. If it were Big Denny, you could hear his heavy breathing for sure, but Marv is in shape. He could be waiting to send you to hell, easy. You stand to the side and try the knob. Locked, but it's nothing but a lock made for bathrooms. A child could defeat that with a straight piece of hanger wire.

You thought hard about how to get into Denny's without getting bushwhacked. One tool you'll need tonight, you already had in your go bag. You thought you might need it to get into the storage locker facility. The other? Super glue. You picked that up at a corner store on the way here.

You take the little cylinder of super glue out of your pocket. You've already cut the tip off the long nose of the plastic cap in the car so you wouldn't have to fuss with it here. Quiet as a smart ninja can be, you run the tip of the cap down the side of the mechanical room door as you squeeze the tube. The glue solidifies almost instantly. You smile. This is one level up from smart ninja and into James Bond territory. Makes you wish life had a movie soundtrack.

Maybe you're acting paranoid and Marv isn't in there, but you would be if you were Marv. Marv is smarter than Harv. Twins aren't really identical. Marv was in better shape and attributed his smarts to being twenty-one minutes older than his brother. "I'm more experienced in the world," Marv joked. Well. The first few times it was a joke. Then he kept saying it.

The super glue might not hold for long, but it would slow Marv down long enough for you to whirl and unload your SIG into him. Satisfied with stage one, you creep down the hallway to Denny's door.

There's no sign of forced entry, as the cops say. You had hoped Marv had come earlier and ransacked the place to find the key and left. From your conversation with Jimmy, it's clear Denny figured out where the key must be. You'd told him as he was beating your ass by the pit, so there's more evidence Denny must still be alive.

Despite everything, you really do hope Denny isn't dead or even hurt badly. You guys have a lot of history behind you. He saved you a few times. He was a good partner. No. More than that, Denny was like a brother right up until he tried to kill you. If you end up having to kill him twice, you will be genuinely upset.

You stop again and listen. The woman upstairs still screams in spasms of anger. It sounds like she's following someone out. Whoever she yells at remains quiet. You can't even hear a murmur under the hysterical woman's cries as she comes down the stairs. "This is it, this time! Don't come back! You come back, the locks will be changed! I'm better off! Don't you look at me! You don't *deserve* to look at me!"

Again, Tia Marta rises, a thought zombie that won't stay dead. The last time you saw her, she kind of sounded like the woman upstairs, though Marta's thick German accent made everything seem more ominous. Of course, with Tia Marta, everything really *was* more ominous.

More screaming as they bang down the stairs.

Just go! I'm trying to hear if there's someone in my ex-best friend's apartment waiting to kill me!

Eventually, you hear the front doors on the ground floor bang shut as the woman follows her ex out. Other guys would have rushed in by now, but you're a smart ninja. You wait next to Denny's door, holding your breath and straining your ears.

You once saw on TV that doctors pitch their hearing when they listen to a patient's heart through a stethoscope so they sense the finer workings, listening for murmurs and catches that spell doom. It sounded like bullshit, but right now, your head cocked and straining, you believe it. Getting through this door might be the key to getting back in control of your destiny. If you get hold of Denny's stash, and if you live through tonight, you could spend the rest of a rich, long life with Lily. Most straight-edge citizens wait for extraordinary things to happen to them. But you? You could make this happen.

There's no sound of a TV or whispered conversation or the clink of a glass. That's good, because the stealth phase of this mission is about to end. You take the second tool out of your trench coat. You've had this stick since you traveled north to Havana on the Hudson.

At first, you were worse off in some ways. You saw snow for the first time in Hudson County, New Jersey. It was colder than you imagined, but you escaped the Bug Man. You were still a scrounging kid on the streets, but you were back among Cubans and Havana on the Hudson felt comforting and familiar. You thought you'd find your mother there. That fantasy sustained you for a long time. If you had stayed in Jersey, you might have grown up to drive a *guagua*, but standing here in your last good suit and a thousand-dollar trench coat, it's hard to imagine living the life of a humble bus driver. Bus drivers can't be Batman, ninjas or James Bond and they don't feel the comforting weight of a SIG Sauer P220 in their pocket. Well, most of them, anyway.

You're not big enough to run at Denny's steel door

and just burst through to toss the place, so you're going to have to make some noise. The tool is a couple of feet of hockey stick. That's the handle. The business end is a bicycle chain. Wrap the chain around any doorknob, use some leverage, wrench it and you're through. The trouble is, you're about to make all the noise you've been avoiding up until this moment.

You have your gun out and ready in case Marv really is about to burst out of the mechanical room. A breach like this is really a two or three-man job to do it right. If you had your druthers, you'd have one guy watching your back and another working the chain around the knob. As long as you're making wishes, it would be best if three guys were taking care of this while you drank mojitos in another state.

No one tries to open the glued door to the equipment room. No one was waiting for you after all. For a moment, you're hot with embarrassment about what a bitch you're being about this. Then you remember your training. The paranoid soldier is the one who survives.

You try to be quiet, but the bicycle chain clinks and clicks and scrapes on Denny's steel door like a slow snare drum. Fuck it. If you can't be ninja stealthy, you'll have to opt for speed. You wrap the chain around the lock and try to open it with one hand. Nope. This is a two-handed job. You stuff the gun in your pocket (guns in belts are for stupid tough guys who shoot their testicles off in the middle of a job.) With two hands, you brace one foot against the frame of the door and haul on the hockey stick handle. The door knob comes away clean and you lean on the door.

Shit. You push with all your weight and the door gaps at the bottom, but there's another lock above where the knob was. You hadn't remembered that one. So much for genius ninja. You look to the apartment across the hall: Apartment D. You step up to that door — it's been quiet over there, too — and you run at Denny's door. Bang! Wow, does your shoulder hurt.

What you wouldn't give for a SWAT team on your side: One of those battering rams for the quick entry, a sledge hammer, a couple of flashbangs and a few canisters of tear gas to plow the way would do nicely. Then you go for old faithful, the ninja stamp. You plant your feet and kick hard, your heel delivering the blow as close to the lock as you can manage. The door swings open with a bang.

An idiot would do a textbook tuck and roll as soon as the door burst in. That's the sort of Hollywood *Beverly Hills Cop* bullshit that will get you shot while you're still trying to roll up into a crouch, still searching for a target in a dark room while your assassin sits in an easy chair with a sawn off in his hands. Tarantino got it right in *Kill Bill*. Uma was the most dangerous assassin in the world but bad old Bud easily bushwhacked her with a shotgun full of rock salt from the comfort of a rocking chair.

As you were messing too long with the door, Marv or Denny could be sitting in the easy chair or on the couch or just on the floor beside the door, the sawn off in his hands already lined up with your chest. You'd hear a boom and the shotgun pellets would tear through you. The hydrostatic shockwave of the punch through your torso would blow a lot of viscera and fluid out through the hole he made. You might have a short flight through the air while you were still figuring out what happened. Then the searing pain would hit you repeatedly, pushing you into the dark.

They say no death is ever instantaneous and the best anyone can hope for is to die in their sleep. The odds of a guy like you dying in your sleep are just about nil, unless you get the ordnance in Denny's stash so you can get the key back from Jimmy Lima. Panama Bob's skim might be the ticket to you dying peacefully in your sleep some day far off, surrounded by children and grandchildren and Lily, old but still somehow beautiful, holding your hand as a nurse pumps up the drugs.

Maybe it will be Propofol, the same shit that let Michael Jackson go in his sleep. You'll go out high and dreaming sweetly instead of gut shot and dying in the doorway of a shitty basement apartment in Washington Heights. The pain and loss will be pushed away by the best drug cocktails that American pharmaceutical companies can supply. Marco was wrong. Baseball isn't the pinnacle of the American Dream. Escaping life painlessly on clean, white sheets is the ultimate goal.

There's no sound from Denny's apartment. Even the mechanical room's hum has gone away. The air feels alive and electric. You aren't just listening with your ears. You reach out with sensors in your skin. You tingle and crackle with life as your heart slams against your ribs.

A smart ninja would take a walk now and come back later. Maybe you could wait by the stairs and see if you can make the other assassin the idiot. Let him pop *his* empty head out around the corner of the door frame to get it shot off. A smart ninja would make whoever's in there chase you out into the hall where the odds are even and you're the guy lying on the floor in wait, presenting a small target in the darkened hallway.

But the sad truth is, you don't consider any of those smarter choices in the moment. Your adrenal glands are kicking out adrenaline and testosterone is seething through your bloodstream.

You slip to the floor on your left shoulder and peek in from the bottom of the open door, your SIG out in front of you. You can't see a thing in there.

Denny's little apartment is as dark as the inside of an ass and smells almost as good. You've been here but you never stayed long. Denny complained the building's water was always too cold so he rarely took showers. You told Denny as sweetly as possible that he gave big sweaty guys a bad name. As you drove around with him and made your rounds for Jimmy and Bob, you rolled down the windows, even in January.

Marv or Denny could still be in there, waiting for you to do something manly and stupid. Then, smart ninja inspiration strikes and you pick up the fallen doorknob. You had an evil DI who pranked a tank crew with a dummy grenade once. The tank driver pissed his pants and another guy came out a hatch so fast he banged his head and knocked himself cold.

You toss the doorknob into Denny's dark apartment. It clanks satisfactorily. "Grenade!"

Nothing. No one is waiting to kill you. Marv must have gone home. You laugh. You even giggle. You reach in the open door and find the light switch. No one is sitting on the couch with a shotgun levelled at your chest. The La-Z-Boy chair is pointed at the television, but neither Denny nor Marv is in it, cradling a machine gun. Getting shot at and almost getting killed has you jumpy and more paranoid than ever, but everything's fine.

Then you stiffen as the cold muzzle comes to rest behind your ear. You aren't a smart ninja. You weren't nearly paranoid enough.

You drop your gun and it hits the floor with a disheartening clunk. It would be embarrassing if it had gone off and shot you through the head, but only briefly. Such a clumsy death would be quite a relief compared to the alternatives that await you. You turn slowly to face the reaper and there's Marv with his precious Tech 9 pointed at your head.

Behind him, the door to Apartment D is open. Behind that, you see the body of a woman on the floor. Marv's been waiting for you so long and so patiently, the blood's drying on the dead woman's floor. A housefly lands on the dead woman's face and drinks deep. Her head sits in the pool of blood. Her eyes are open. Her look is accusing. Her face, drenched red from her vicious head wound, is a chilling combination of *I'm not really surprised* and *You're next, you prideful idiot, you useless tool. You're no better than your father.*

THE GAMBLER

"The little Cuban," Marv says. "You're ten feet of trouble in a 5'9" sack of shit."

Your eyes are still fixed on the dead woman's face. "You didn't have to do that, Marv. What did she ever do to you? She was a civilian."

"Collateral damage," he says.

"I never liked that term. It's jargon. It's a term made up by bureaucrats and press secretaries to cover up killing innocent people. You and me, we're not innocent, but that lady was. When Denny was sick last Christmas, she brought him baked beans and gave him an ice pack for the fever. He told me. Her name was...was Mrs. D. Denny could never remember her name but it began with a D and she was from apartment D so that's how Denny remembered that much."

Marv digs the Tech 9's muzzle into your sternum and you step back. In the movies, the hero grabs for the gun or kicks it out of the gunner's fist. That's stupid. Try anything fancy and Marv will tighten up. He might not even mean to shoot you — yet — but that won't be much comfort as you bleed out on

Denny's dirty rug. Hand-to-hand combat is for when both guys' guns are empty. Even then, it's much better to fight just long enough to go find more ammo and reload.

Time to go into lying and negotiation mode. "Can we talk, or," you nod at his gun, "is this going to be a short conversation?"

Marv gestures with the gun and you sit in the La-Z-boy.

"I can't wait to tell the guys about you throwing that doorknob and pretending it was a grenade. Hilarious, man."

"You saw that, huh?"

"All through the peephole."

"It'll be a good story. You want to hear another?"

Marv doesn't miss a beat. "Are you going to tell me about where the key to Panama Bob's skim is or are you going to give me that same bullshit story about how Bob was into some crazy counterfeiting scheme with Freejack Jack?"

You blink. "I was going to try the bullshit story about counterfeiting, actually."

Marv smiles wider, like the corners of his mouth might get caught up in his ears. "Yeah, see that worked great on Pete. One, because you can sell a story, and two, because Pete's greed is bigger than his brains. That's saying something because Pete's pretty smart. But I worked for Bob. I knew about the skim, but he slipped us enough, Harv and me, that we could keep our traps shut."

You settle into the chair. It's best not to look too freaked out with Marv waving the gun your way. If he is going to shoot, you may as well go out acting cool. You're genuinely afraid the doorknob as hand grenade story might be your legacy. You've got a lot to live down. Sure, you looked like an idiot, but you'd have been a genius if the ploy had flushed out a bushwhacker.

Keeping the Tech 9 on you, Marv walks backwards and closes Mrs. D's door. When he comes back in, he closes Denny's door and paces back and forth. "How about I tell you a story for a change?"

You shrug. It might give you some time to say a few Hail Marys. "Sure."

"Once upon a time there was a traveling poker game. Different place every week. High rollers. Sometimes in the back of a restaurant, all night long. Sometimes at somebody's house in the suburbs, out among the civilians with their barbecues and 2.5 kids and picket fences. Could be anywhere, but this one night, it's in the back of Con Carnies. You know this story? It's an oldie but a goodie."

You shake your head, hoping it's a good long story because you've just discovered you can't remember a single phrase beyond "Hail Mary, full of grace."

"One of the guys who works in the back of Carnies? He was a dishwasher. He overheard the boss talk about how these underworld types were coming in after midnight for a high stakes poker night. There's going to be thousands of dollars on the table. Maybe a hundred thousand. Maybe even more. And this little dishwasher starts getting ideas. He starts to think about how his life sucks and if he had that kind of money...if he made one bold move? Well, he wouldn't be a dishwasher anymore, would he? Maybe he could take his girl and escape to Miami, huh?"

Sweat trickles down your neck while jagged ice

turns in your stomach.

"This dishwasher gets big ideas about himself. He gets a plan together. He figured if he could crash that poker game, he could steal all that money and he'd get away free. They're a bunch of bad dudes around that table, but there's one good thing about robbing bad dudes. They can't very well call the cops, can they? He figures, with that kind of money, he can disappear far enough down a hole, he won't get tracked down. It sounds like a good plan, doesn't it? Does it remind you of anyone, Jesus, you stupid fuck?"

"No, but keep talking. You're exciting me. Sexually."

"Heh. Smart mouth on a dumb guy. *Grenade!*" Marv laughs and then settles in, his eyes never leaving yours. "The little dishwasher realizes he should probably have some muscle. Bad dudes carrying big cash will be armed, for sure. They might even have bodyguards in the room to complicate things. He knows he's got to go in hard, but he can't bring himself to get anybody else in on the scheme because more guys means more mouths to talk and more mouths to feed afterward. He doesn't want to split the cash up. That would screw up the point of his gamble."

"Right."

"Which reminds me, did you even check on Denny after you threw him into that hole? Or did you just leave him to die? Pretty cold way to treat a partner."

"Did Denny tell you why he ended up in the hole?"

Marv pauses. "That's kind of the point of my story, Jesus. You screwed yourself by betraying Denny, by being so greedy you didn't want to share the skim with anybody."

You shrug. "The way I see it, he betrayed me. He did try to kill me and he gave me this mug." You gesture to your face.

"Denny says different."

You now have confirmation: Denny is alive. Not surprisingly, in Denny's version of the story, he wasn't giving up that he was sleeping with Jimmy's wife. Interesting. You think you can use that, but then Marv tells you the rest and that little burning hope is extinguished.

"The little dishwasher gets an idea that he should go in hard with a machine gun. That's a good instinct, but his trouble is, he's still a dishwasher. He doesn't know anything. Where's he going to find a machine gun on a few hours' notice? But, he figures, this is the Bronx. If you can't scare up some serious hardware in the Bronx, it's not the Bronx, right? So he asks his buddies and phone calls are made but the best anybody can do is to give him a double-barrelled twelve gauge. You want an M-16? Come back tomorrow. You want an Uzi? Sure, but not till next week. Plus, all that didn't matter because, like I said, he's a dishwasher. He can't afford to pay for major ordnance. He's only got enough scratch for the shotgun and he's lucky it's not a little squirrel gun."

Denny said you knocked him into the pit so he couldn't be in on the skim. Does *Pete* know this isn't about fake bills, yet? He must, if Marv knows. In which case, you're screwed twice. Again.

"Hey! Am I boring you? Can I shoot you now?"

"Nah, I'm riveted. Shoot me at the end."

"Agreed. Where was I?"

"Dishwasher with a twelve gauge. Big dreams. Gets

the money. Escapes. Lives happily ever after because that's how all mob stories end."

"Heh. I'm going to almost miss you."

But Marv won't miss with that Tech 9.

"Dishwasher with a twelve gauge comes into the room hard. He's all hyped up. The underworld types are appropriately surprised anyone could be so galactically dumb that he thinks he can rob them and not end up with his nuts getting roasted for breakfast. Still, for a whole minute there, the little guy is large and in charge, as we used to say back in the day. He rushes in and bodyguards are there, but he owns them and this little guy gets that first charge of power. Probably the first charge he had since he discovered his own dick. He jumps up on the poker table and screams, 'All you motherfuckers put your dough on the table!' And just to emphasize his point, he lets go with the scattergun and puts a hole in the ceiling. Clearly, the little dishwasher is bone crazy."

"Clearly."

"So these wise guys mutter and scowl, but they pony up and start putting wads of cash on the table. Wads of it, man. More money than the dishwasher has seen in his tiny life. He gets all excited. About then, the guy realizes he doesn't have anything to put all the money in. A pillowcase or a big garbage bag would have done the job easy, but he didn't think it through. There's all this money for the taking, if only he can get out the door."

"What's he do? Talk slow. I'm getting horny."

Marv gives a genuine smile. "You may not like how I punctuate the period when I say 'The End'. Anyway, the little guy is screaming for somebody to give him something to put all the money in. And the gangsters around the table? They really can't help it. This guy is screaming and jumping around and one of them laughs a little. It's just obvious it's amateur hour. The guy doesn't know what he's doing. Nobody's brought a bag to the back of the restaurant. There's no briefcase full of cash. What did the guy expect? Amateurs always think they're going to bulldog their way in and figure it out once they're in there. It's crazy time. The theft doesn't begin and end with getting a gun. You gotta have a brain behind the trigger."

You think what a happy coincidence it would be if Marv had a brain aneurysm just then. That would be ironic and helpful. Maybe if you could remember all the words to the Hail Mary, whatever psycho is in charge of the universe would give you a break. You close your eyes, make an earnest wish, and snap them open in a hard blink. Nope, Marv still looks remarkably healthy. Harv did say Marv worked out a lot.

"So this little dishwasher gets pissed off because what started as a chuckle spreads around the room. 'Gimme something to put this money in! Gimme something to put all your money in!' And the wise guys just start to laugh harder. That only pisses off the little guy more. They ain't taking him seriously. That's the one thing on earth nobody can stand for long. So the dishwasher? He screams louder! And then, just to make sure they see his point of view, you know, for emphasis? He fires off another cartridge into the ceiling! Just to make his point! You see the problem?"

"It was a double-barrelled shotgun. He's out of ammo."

Marv touches his index finger to his nose.

"The wise guys all stop laughing at once and everybody round the table, the bodyguards, even a couple of the hookers, according to legend...they all pull out their gats and take a bead on the idiot. He doesn't show up for work again, you know what I mean?"

"I like that story. Would you like to tell me a few more, say until the sun explodes? I can wait."

"Heh-heh. You just get one, but do you know the point of the story, Mr. Diaz?"

"Observe the golden rule? Temper your ambition? It's always darkest right before everything gets really fucked up?"

Marv gives you another genuine smile. How he does it, it's creepy. "My point is, you're that guy and you've shot your wad. You gave Pete some story about counterfeit cash that got him to hold off on killing you. That's one shot in the ceiling."

"In my defence, I was also avoiding torture at the time and I was improvising."

"And you had the key to the skim and you lost it."

"If I'd had it on me, I'm pretty sure Denny would have beaten it out of me. Like, even if I'd swallowed it. Like I said, I was improvising at the time."

"Uh-huh. The upshot is, you're out of stories. Jimmy wanted you to know that he knows you're fulla shit. Pete knows there's no counterfeit scheme that will make him the new boss and he's not going to clear Jimmy Lima out of the way. You've got nothing left to bargain with."

He raises the Tech 9 and you sense the straight line of the energetic connection between the muzzle and the spot in the middle of your forehead where the bullet will drill in. "And we've come to the period after The End."

"I might have one thing."

"No, thanks, Jesus. I enjoyed our chat, though. You were a funny guy."

"Do you know who killed your brother?" you ask.

His hand tightens around the gun. If the Tech 9 had a hair trigger, it would have bucked in his hand by now and you'd already be dead. You close your eyes and count to three. You're going to live, maybe another moment longer. You heard on some morning radio trivia show once that the technical definition of a *moment* is just 90 seconds long.

"Harv is...dead?" Marv asks. "Who did it? Was it you?" He raises his gun again.

You shake your head vigorously. You can't tell him it was Lily, but there are plenty of people you hate on whom you can throw blame like flaming napalm. "Jake did it. On Jimmy's orders."

"You're lying. That's all you do."

"Have you heard from Harv?"

Marv's eyes flicker and, for the first time, three deep worry lines appear on his forehead.

"I killed Panama Bob on Jimmy's orders because Bob was skimming and Jimmy wants to own The Machine. Jimmy obviously wants me dead because I know about the skim and Jimmy wants it all. I was supposed to get it, or the key to it, anyway, before I whacked Bob. I didn't expect him to go crazy ass and run out the window onto a ledge and hide behind a gargoyle. Jimmy assumed the skim would be on the premises. Now that Jimmy's got the key to the skim, he wants everybody who knows about it dead. That's me, Denny, Harv and you."

Marv lowers the gun and pulls out his cell phone. It rings and rings. At least it does on Marv's end of the line. On Harv's end, maybe it's burbling underwater somewhere deep and dark. When his twin fails to answer, Marv grows another worry line. He gives you snake eyes. "You have a history of bullshit."

"Let me dial Jake. If I'm lying, you can shoot me in the balls."

Marv's eyebrows shoot up. After a short pause he says, "Respect." He presses the key on his cell for speaker phone and hands it to you.

You dial Jake and he answers on the first ring. "Jake! They already found Harv's body! You moron! What did you do? You don't know your job, man!"

"Bullshit!" Jake says. "He's never going to pop up. Where'd you hear different? And why are you talking this shit on a c—?"

You close the cell and hand it back to Marv.

"Bastard!" Marv cries.

You look away and study the carpet to give him a few minutes to grieve.

When he quietens, you clear your throat. "Harv and I were talking about a truce so we could combine forces and go after Jimmy. He won't stop until anyone who knows anything about his power grab or the skim is dead. You know that."

Marv tosses his handgun onto the couch cushion beside him and buries his face in his hands, holding nothing back. You'd cry, too. Harv had that *H* tattoo on his neck and Marv has his matching *M*. As muscle, a team of identical twins, they did look pretty cool, like a couple of heavies out of a Bond movie. Without Harv, Marv's just another douche nozzle with a neck tattoo.

"Jake's gonna die for killing my brother and Jimmy's gotta die for giving the order," Marv says.

"Then you better let me live so I can help you. You're going to need me if you're going to storm the castle. You don't want to run in there without enough firepower like some amateur dishwasher."

"Valid," he says. His face still in his hands, he asks in a small voice, "What do we do for firepower?"

"Denny keeps his arsenal behind you in the kitchen. That big freezer doesn't work as a freezer. It's all in there."

When Marv composes himself, he looks up at you with puffy red eyes, looking like the little boy he must have been at some point. We're all little boys. Sometimes, in moments like these, it leaks out.

"Jimmy's got some guys on high alert," Marv says. "How are we going to get to him?"

You consider that a moment and an idea forms. It's not a good one, but it's all you've got. "Your job is to find me and maybe get the locker location for the key, right?"

"The main thing was to kill you, though." He shrugs. "Up until a few minutes ago, anyway, but the idiot little Cuban enemy of my enemy is my friend."

"Did you call them to let them know I was here?"

"Of course not. I wasn't going to give away my position and give up my front row seat to the grenade thing."

"Yeah, yeah. Stop bustin' balls. My point is, as far as Jimmy's concerned, you're still on Team Lima, right?"

Marv gives you a reaper's smile. "Yeah, Machine-ready."

"Then I got a way into the castle. No idea how we'll get out, but there's a safe way in."

"Safe?"

"Safe-ish."

"Rock it, Rocket. Lay it out for me."

THE ULTIMATE LIAR

"Paper or plastic?" Bug Man asks. In his mirrored sunglasses, you hardly recognize yourself. You have never seen yourself in terror. Terror makes your face longer. Your hands are tied to the rail of his boat. He can do anything he wants. When the Captain struck your father with the butt of his rifle, there was no time for hatred. When the Captain threw your father overboard, there was only room for fear. Later, you hated the sea, but even then, you knew that it was nature. Nature is not personal. But there is time to hate the Bug Man. There will be much time to discover new depths of loathing.

"Are you going to be a good boy? Good boys get paper."

You piss yourself and the yellow puddle wets the Bug Man's leather deck shoes.

"Bad boy." He slips a clear plastic bag over your head. "I own you. You belong to me."

Your face is hot and the bag tightens, wrapping your face in a transparent shroud. You didn't have time to hold your breath. You want to scream but that's a waste of breath. Your vision fills with black spots. At first you're afraid, but soon you welcome the nonexistence the spots bring. The black spots grow large to meet each other to build infinite darkness. You are dead and the Bug Man can only kill you once.

No, you aren't that lucky.

When you wake in the dark, you feel small. Your body aches. The Bug Man pushed you down the stairs. You sort of remember that: flight, like when your father threw you into the air to land in the water of the shallow end of the hotel pool he was supposed to be cleaning. Then you realize you were not flying but falling and the pain came. You crashed, banging and scraping against the jagged edges of rough wooden stairs to the cold, concrete floor. You are in the basement of what must be a large house and there is someone here with you.

You pray to Jesus. You ask the Virgin Mother for help. You ask God if it's an angel breathing in the dark. (Do angels breathe, or are they more like fish? Are they more like divine birds with gills? You hope so.)

The angel listens to you until you tire of asking God for the same thing over and over: Deliver you from evil and give you your family back. As the silence stretches out, the angel moves, shuffling. The only light is a line under the door at the top of the stairs. Moving to the stairs, the silhouette reveals himself. He is a boy, older than you, or at least bigger. As soon as he speaks, you are crushed again. God, Jesus and the Virgin Mary would understand you. They would speak kind and comforting words, but this boy speaks in English. You don't, not yet.

God has turned his back on you, even though you are named for his only begotten son. "For God so loved the world, he sent his only begotten son..." God the Father didn't send help when Christ was on the cross. You never understood that, but you think of your mother's Bible lessons and the fear is fresh. If God didn't send help for Jesus Christ suffering on the cross, he probably won't send an army of angels to rescue Jesus Salvador Umberto Luis Diaz.

The boy chatters on. It's gibberish. He repeats something and you pick it out of the torrent of English words. You ask him to speak slower, not to understand, but to commit the words to memory in case you live to understand more later. Maybe he understands you a little, or maybe he just repeats the same thing, like he's praying, too. He says the words into the night because God's not listening. The boy says the same words until you're sure you will never forget. That night, you dream your first English words: "My name is Darren Hill and I'm from Sarasota. If you try to run away, they'll kill me. I'm next. I'm next! I'm next! I'm next!"

Bright, white lights behind cages of thin wire mesh blaze on, dazzling you. A tall woman with her hair pinned high on the back of her head clacks down the wooden stairs carrying a silver tray. Before she is two steps down, the heavy metal door swings fast on tight springs and slams shut behind her with a click. She puts the tray on a portable table against one wall. The basement isn't as large as you imagined. The walls are cushioned with a padding you soon learn is soundproofed. In the dark, you had been too afraid to explore the dimensions of your prison.

"I am Tia Marta." The woman speaks in Spanish, but with a German accent you had heard from some guests around the hotel in Cuba. "If you behave, there will be rewards. Wonderful rewards. If not? Not."

Your mother read fairy tales at bedtime. Evil kings held princes in dark chambers. Evil witches trapped princesses in high towers. The Bug man imprisoned you in his dungeon. Tia Marta cast a spell. You never knew if she drugged you with the chicken sandwich or the milk.

Before you finish eating, your body slows until it feels like a single blink could be measured with a watch. You slip to the floor and stare as Tia Marta turns the white boy around to show you the danger. Across his buttocks and back are lines. Some are old and healed. Many are fresh slashes of angry red welts.

The first English words you learned were: *sir, mistress, yes, please and thank you.* Tia Marta told you in Spanish that was all you'd need to know for the first few weeks. She didn't add "...until you are broken." You learned that later, too.

The word *no* is not a word you are permitted to utter. They beat you until you understand. They take away your name, too. You are not a person. You are just a boy, which is the same as being a thing like a lamp or a dishrag. Tia Marta and the Bug Man make clear in English, Spanish and with their fists and whips: Things can be thrown away easily.

You run your finger down the list of vocabulary words. Each time your Spanish accent creeps in, Tia Marta corrects you with a sharp rap of her ruler across your knuckles.

"After the age of nineteen, it's all over," she says. You aren't sure what Tia Marta is talking about but you nod earnestly. "There's a switch in the brain. After a certain age you don't get any taller and you can't talk like a native speaker anymore. Arnold Schwarzenegger came here from Austria to become the American dream, but he still got here just a little too late to lose the accent. Once it's bred in the bone, it doesn't come out. He still says '*Cully-fornia*' and 'red vine and vite vine' not 'red wine and white wine.' You're lucky, boy. The Sir brought me to this country too late. I was twenty. A little earlier and I could be speaking English like a Southern belle. Wouldn't that be charming?"

"Yes, mistress." You speak up clearly or she'll slap you.

"But my accent is pretty as it is, isn't it?"

"Yes, mistress." But not too loud or she'll slap you so hard, her fingers will leave a red outline on your cheek. Or she'll use her long fingernails and leave a mark, like she does more and more with the other boy.

"I'm very pleased with the progress in your attitude, boy."

"Yes, mistress. Thank you, mistress." Like the story Tia Marta told you of the Medusa, you must never look her in the eye. And you must never, ever, look too long at the key on the heavy gold chain that hangs from Tia Marta's neck.

"Good boy. So good, in fact, I think you're ready for some training. I've waited long enough. How about we watch a movie you'll like? You are going to love this. It's an old one called *Fast Times at Ridgemount High*. To improve your English, listen to the actors' diction and pay particular attention to the girl in the red bikini."

"Yes, mistress."

You don't understand the jokes and you're afraid to laugh at the wrong times, so you smile for Tia Marta. Then the pretty girl in the red bikini opened the front of her bikini top to show her breasts. Tia Marta reaches for you, her long fingers pushing into your lap, grasping and clawing as you squeal. You are so shocked you stand as if you could leave. Tia Marta is so upset, she calls the Sir.

The Bug Man strides in wearing a three-piece powder blue suit. He is especially angry because you interrupted a business call. He has to take off his jacket and vest to give you what he calls "a proper punishment." He leaves big splotches of purple bruises that take weeks to finally yellow. Tia Marta slashes her long nails across your chest.

Under terrible circumstances, time passes so very slowly.

Finally..."Paper or plastic?"

Paper is just for scaring you and keeping you off-balance and clueless as to where you are and when the next blow will come. Plastic is near-death, or at least it has been so far. You've learned to gauge his moods and there isn't a chance he'll put a paper bag over your head tonight.

For the first time, you answer bravely, "Plastic, Sir! And please don't stop. Use the plastic bag and don't stop!"

But you aren't that lucky. The countless days and awful nights melt into each other and for the rest of your time with Tia Marta and the Bug Man, you are no longer allowed the dignity of clothing, just like Darren Hill from Sarasota.

"You are my smartest and best student, boy."

"Thank you, mistress."

"You've earned your new place."

You don't know what she means until Darren Hill from Sarasota, your companion in the dark for three years, disappears. You didn't try to run away, but the Bug Man took him anyway. Darren was growing into a man and so Tia Marta is done with him.

One night, soon after Darren's exit, a little boy crashes down the wooden stairs to the floor. The light from under the door catches the boy's terrified face for just a moment. He cries out and babbles in Spanish how he is afraid and he begs you to take him home. You hold him and rock him. This is...familiar. In the dark, the boy is as small as Rodolpho. You beg him not to cry. "If you cry, Tia Marta and the Bug Man might come down here."

You haven't been allowed to speak Spanish for a long time but, to calm the boy, you risk it and, once spoken, you find you can't stop. "My name is Jesus Salvador Umberto Luis Diaz and I am from Cuba. Don't try to run away or they'll kill me. I'm next. I'm next!"

Footsteps.

"Sh! Sh! Please, shut up. Please!"

The footsteps are sharp and fast. That's not the Bug Man. His step is heavy and slower. Tia Marta almost always wears high heels and sometimes she uses them in terrible, painful ways.

"Please be quiet! *Sh! Rodolpho!*"

And there it is. Rodolpho. You have cried for your brother many nights after the lights were out, but you have not spoken his name since the day you tried to save him and, instead, the water turned a frothy pink.

Tia Marta moves around in the kitchen, close enough to hear your words, but you can't stop crying and the boy won't stop crying and you can't stop saying, "Rodolpho! His name was *Rodolpho*! My father's name was Marco and my mother's was Maritza and I am Jesus Salvador Umberto Luis Diaz! I am here, Rodolpho! I am Jesus Salvador Umberto Luis Diaz! I am Jesus Salvador Umberto Luis Diaz!"

The lights blaze on. Tia Marta clacks down the stairs carrying the silver tray. The door swings, slams and clicks behind her. The boy is a slight kid with a bowl haircut. He looks surprised at your naked body, or maybe it's the criss-crossed scars that shock him more.

"Boys, boys, boys! There has been a fracture of decorum in the Sir's house."

Tia Marta puts the tray of food on the little table and, with an expansive gesture and a cunning smile, she invites the little boy to eat the food. Then she turns to you and her smile fades to a thin, hard line. "A fracture deserves a fracture, don't you agree, boy?"

"I am Jesus Salvador Umberto Luiz Diaz."

"I heard those words. I thought we'd beaten them out of you. I thought you were grateful."

You test the forbidden word: "No."

"What did you say to me? Aren't you still my little boy?"

"No."

She comes at you, nails slashing for your eyes, clawing for your throat.

You leap back in fear and try to run. The first strike isn't the cut of her nails or a blazing slap but a hard thrust to your jaw with the heel of her hand that sends you reeling.

"Don't worry, Jesus! I'm going to beat that name out of you and you *will* be grateful again. I'll squeeze you like a pimple. I put you down so hard you won't even *remember* your name." She swings at you again and you feel the wind of her dangerous arc past your eyes. "And I'm doing it all for love. Of all the playthings the Sir has given me, you have survived the longest and I'm not done with you yet! You aren't a man yet. You've got a few miles left in you. I want more! Only when I decide you've earned it, do you get plastic for the last time."

You duck under her next swing, infuriating her.

"Remember, this isn't a beating, little boy! I'm *training* you!"

The little kid cowers in a corner, covering his face with his hands. His cheeks are wet. He's praying, but you've already tried that so many times, any hope and power your prayers might have had is drained.

You need a weapon. The plastic cups and the paper plate Tia Marta brought down here are useless, but the silver tray has weight. She follows your gaze and lunges to stop you. You avoid her, but not for long. Her arms come around your neck from behind and you know what comes next. Black spots. Later you'll wake up, naked and staked down. The torture will begin.

She's choking you out, but your left hand fumbles for the tray. You fumble. You reach. You miss. She's taller and stronger and outweighs you by at least forty pounds. Your hands reach for her arms but she's wrapped around your throat, tightening and squeezing like a python. Her hands are fists so you can't grab at her fingers to try to pry her off. You've imagined gouging out her eyes a thousand times, but now you're flailing and failing.

You're out of air.

You kick at the tray table, hoping to pop the silver tray up into your hands. Instead, you only succeed in kicking the tray away from you farther. You've risked everything and lost.

Tia Marta is laughing in your ear. It's a cruel sound, like there's metal in her throat. Despite all the anatomical similarities with which you're familiar from the vast amount of sadistic pornography she's shown you, you suspect Tia Marta is not human.

"I'm going to make it last, boy!"

You're losing the world. The black curtain is coming down and when the curtain comes up again and you reluctantly surface into the light, the physics of the world will end. The earth will rotate slower, almost to a stop, as Tia Marta explores the nerves of your skin in exquisite detail. "Nociceptors," she calls them. "The pain nerves. Even more fun than the nerves we use for pleasure."

Time will slow as the torture begins. She might

take so long, all the clocks on the planet will stop.

"Tómelo!" Take it!

The little boy slides the cool silver tray into your sweating palms. You're so weak without air you almost drop it, but something more is still left. Your hands are rigid claws. You slam the tray behind your head in blind desperation.

The edge of the heavy tray slams into Tia Marta's face. She won't let go, not yet. And surprise! That is a *good* thing. You twist your chin to try to pry under the blade of her forearm. You slam the heavy tray into her face again and you suck in air through your nose even as you sink your teeth into the meat of her arm.

She shrieks, lets go, stumbles back, but not without a ripping sound. Her eyes go huge as she stares at the gash pumping blood from her wounded arm. You spit the meat to the ground in front of her and she looks at you with...is that...*glee*? She is not human. Shaking, bleeding, smiling, Tia Marta reaches up with the arm that is whole and draws out one of the long, sharp pins that holds her hair up and points it at your eyes. "This will be a fine demonstration for my new playmate!"

She lunges at your eyes and you use the tray as a shield, deflecting her thrust up while you kick out as hard as you can, nailing her in the belly and doubling her over. The hairpin spins away as you knock her arm to to the side. You bring the edge of the heavy, silver tray down on her neck. It's as if God has wished away all her bones. She is a heap on the floor. But you keep hammering at her head with the tray, punctuating each savage blow with your newfound words: "I! Am! Jesus! Salvador! Umberto! Luis!

Diaz!"

You're crying as you grab the chain around her exposed neck and strangle her to make sure she has nothing left. You can't be sure. Tia Marta only *looks* human. You open your eyes when you feel the little boy's cool, shaking hands on yours, gently pulling you away from the thing on the cold concrete.

The Bug Man was out of the house, away on business. His clothes are too big for you, but you'll grow into them some day and when you do, fine suits by Armani will conceal your scars.

You and the boy head north and you don't stop running until you get to Havana on the Hudson. The boy thought he'd find his parents there but he never did. Instead, the little boy becomes your new brother, Little Denny De Molina. When he gets to be Big Denny De Molina, he'll save you. He'll get you into The Machine after you come back from Iraq with a dishonourable discharge.

You've been telling yourself the man you pushed to his death in a construction pit was just a friend. You are such a good liar, you lied to yourself the most and the best. Big Denny was always more than a friend. But he's alive and you're afraid you're going to have to kill him again, if he doesn't murder you first, of course.

THE WAY OUT IS THROUGH

When you walk in, Lily's in bed but still in her dress, the bed covers pulled up to her breasts. Lily's drinking rum and Coke, sort of. She tips back the rum, gulping straight from the bottle and, once she's made room, adds some soda and gives it a gentle swirl. She'll be plastered long before it's all Coca-Cola.

You close the door, peer out through a gap in the curtains and watch to make sure you haven't been followed.

"You pick up a tail? You got a shadow? You worried you're going to get whacked?"

"Don't talk like that."

"Why? Does it sound dumb when I say it?"

You turn from the window. "I just don't want you to jinx us."

"Why not? I'm a moll now, aren't I? I killed one of Jimmy Lima's soldiers. That's something. Lily in the library with a candlestick! Lily in the conservatory with the lead pipe! Lily in the living room with a big ol' frying pan! Lily swings for the fences! I thought I'd never get sucked into Dad's world. I had plans. I was going to go to Paris and study art. I was going to be one of those girls. Berets and books and Euro passes for the trains and backpacking."

You sag. "I guess you shouldn't have gone slumming with the help then, huh?"

"Don't be petulant, Jesus. It's not sexy."

You reach for the bottle but she frowns and holds it to her chest. "Mine."

You retrieve a little plastic cup from the bathroom and unwrap it from its paper sheath. You hold out the glass and Lily pours you a couple of fingers. Your drink tastes stiff. You sit on the bed and watch her throat as she tilts her head back and swallows.

"How did you find out Pete does what he does?"

Lily shrugs. "Lots of little girls and boys don't know or care what their parents do for a living. For a long time, all anybody in the family said was that Dad was a businessman. You get that early enough, you don't question it. The mob's like religion. You get in early enough, the weird doesn't feel weird."

"And later?"

"I wasn't a dumb kid. I had an inkling. One time, over Christmas dinner — maybe I was twelve — Dad toasted 'the suckers'. I asked in front of everybody who the suckers were and the men laughed and the women got quiet. Mom told me Dad's business was trading stocks. Mom wanted to keep me in the dark forever. She kept up the pretence of Santa Claus and the Easter Bunny long after I found out where Christmas presents and Easter eggs come from. Friends from school told me the truth about the Easter Bunny and Santa. I didn't tell her I knew the truth because I *liked* the presents. If I said I didn't believe, the presents would have stopped."

"When did you know Pete was connected for sure?"

"I began to get it over time. I knew Dad was important, how other guys talked to him. When he met a client in the street, they were extra nice to him, like he was their boss or a kind of celebrity or something. I started to get it watching guys like Jake. The way those young guys defer to him, like they respect him, but they fear him, too. Fear is easy to spot. It's everywhere."

"What did Pete say when you figured it out?"

"I'd known for a while but I had the mob talk with him when I turned sixteen. I asked him to tell me about his business."

"He said his business wasn't any of my business because he put food on the table. Almost ruined that sweet sixteen party." She takes another long swallow.

Lily's hair is mussed and hangs over half her face. Her red lipstick is smeared and uneven. She looks sexier than ever.

"Mom took me aside and told me Dad was in the gambling business, that it was technically illegal, but it wasn't bad. It was only illegal because the government doesn't want competition for all its own gambling and lotto schemes."

"So you didn't make a scene at your sweet sixteen?"

"No, I did with Daddy what I did with Santa Claus and the Easter Bunny. I chose the presents."

"You chose your family. That's not so bad. I wish I had that option."

"Is this finally the moment where we open up to each other, bare our souls and you tell me why you never want to take your clothes off to have sex?"

"I like my clothes."

"You do take them off, right? Like to shower, I mean."

"Of course — !"

"Chillax, Jesus. I'm only picking at you. You're an exotic scab, you are."

You drink. You don't like the taste, but it's better than talking. Why does anyone have to talk at all?

"So why don't you want to get naked with me? Are you covering up embarrassing tattoos? From what you've let me see, you don't seem to have any tattoos. I was thinking you had an ex-girlfriend's tattoo on you somewhere and you're worried it will piss me off."

"Would it piss you off?"

"No. Of course not."

Not the answer you were hoping for. "What if I have dozens of tattoos all over from my exes?"

She laughs and takes a long drink. "You? I don't think so, Jesus. The way you are, I don't think there are a lot of girls in your history. You're the kind of guy who thinks he has to be in love to have sex."

It hurts you, how true this is. Your first sexual experience wasn't just loveless. It was hate-filled. Love and Armani are insulation from those memories. "Staying in the suit hasn't stopped us from doing anything," you say.

"A girl gets skin hunger, Jesus. It's not just about getting off. It's about the closeness, too...at least when it's good."

You shrug and have another drink, waiting for a new conversation thread to pull. You can feel her eyes on your neck.

"Fear is easy to spot," she says, slurring her words.

"I said that before, right?"

"Yeah. How are *you* doing with fear, Lily? You killed Harv. You doing okay with that?"

She jiggles the bottle at you. "I'm dealing with it. What about you? Who was the first person you killed?"

"I'm not going to talk about that." But the mere question raises the spectre of a scream cut short and pink water in whirling blades. You push that thought away with another. "I'm more worried about the last person I killed. I thought I got Denny, but he's still around, and probably very angry with me."

"Okay. You thought you killed Denny but he lived. Who was before that?"

You can't tell her you threw Panama Bob off a ledge. He's still Uncle Bobby to her. You hold out your cup and wait for her to pour. She does and you knock this one back.

"You're afraid," she says. "Why can't you tell me anything? I took a frying pan to Harv's head. I've earned my bones. Did a good job of it, too. The Machine should have an equal opportunity employment policy. I could be an enforcer."

"Yeah," you say. "You've got an air about you that's definitely *Kill Bill.*"

"What is it with you and movies? Start with that. I just saved your life and we're on the run and I don't really know what the fuck is going on, so how about you tell me? We could have a real conversation. We've had fun. Then I killed a guy for you. We should really move on to the next step in our relationship and have a serious discussion, don't you think?"

You tell her you'll solve all the problems. You tell

her you'll take care of her and she doesn't have to worry anymore and she'll never get any blame for Harv's death. You tell her it's better if she doesn't know. You say anything you can to placate her, to shut her up and to make her stop asking you questions. And her answer is to cry, dig under the covers and hand you a newspaper.

It's on the front page of the City section. A bomb killed Derek "Cob" Cobzaru, a Romanian mobster from Washington Heights yesterday afternoon. His two children, a boy and girl aged six and eight, were also in the car when it blew up. "I caught some of what Harv said. He said Uncle Jimmy was making up that the Romanians killed Uncle Bob. He said something about how he was trying to throw blame. Did Jimmy really make the order for Bob to die?"

"I guess so."

"You guess so? What does that mean, you guess so?"

"It means I want to tell you as much or as little as it takes to keep you calm."

She sneers.

"And to keep you out of this as much as I can. The less you know, the better for you."

"The Romanian guy. His kids were little, Jesus. Suffer the little children. You know what this means? It's war. The Machine is supposed to be about making money. How is a gang war going to help that? And how am I supposed to keep calm? I've known where Dad's money came from since that not-so-sweet sixteen, but I never thought about anybody getting killed."

"Things get complicated." You're beginning to lose the thread. How much has Lily really heard? What does she suspect? How long was Harv in her apartment before you showed up? Did they have long to talk? Did Harv say anything that points Bob's death straight at you instead of Big Denny? Could Lily forgive you if she knew? How much longer can you keep all the lies straight? And why did you drink so much before you got lost in the lies? Is it because the truth is too heavy to carry and you just need to lay it down?

She looks in your eyes. "What's your part? What exactly do you do? Tell me."

"Mostly? I threaten people to make sure they pay up."

"That doesn't sound so bad, but I don't really know, do I? You ever kill a little kid? You won't fuck me without one of your precious suits on. What else goes on behind your eyes? How deep does the sickness go?"

You close your eyes. "I don't kill civilians. If I show up on somebody's doorstep coming heavy, they're already dirty and brought it on themselves. I don't do car bombs. I am not an indiscriminate monster who kidnaps kids. I've killed people. You know that. But I'm not killing anybody who's in danger of curing cancer. They're all lowlifes. If I show up, they're probably already rotten."

"So you've got a code. Good for you. It's better than none. What about Dad? Has he got a code?"

"Everybody's got a code. Pete's got a code of silence and loyalty. He'd die for Vincent, but he knows Jimmy isn't worth that sacrifice. And Pete would rather stick a knife in his eye than be a rat. That's pretty standard."

"What's his policy on hurting people?"

"The other night when you drove me over to your Dad's place? Pete threatened to burn my balls with cigarettes and he would have if I didn't tell him something he wanted to hear. That's the kind of business your father's in. That's where your car and your apartment and everything else comes from. That's where studying art in Paris and Spain was going to come from."

Lily goes gray. She sits back and drinks some more. There's not much left to drink. It's quiet for a long time. When she speaks again, she sounds different. She sounds like a woman who has grown older. "Thank you for telling me the truth. All this time, I thought I was so smart. I thought it was just about taking bets, like Dad just really loved sports and that was as far as it went."

You drain your cup and hold it out again but she's shaking too much to pour and you take the bottle from her before she can drop it and drink the last. It's all Coca-Cola now.

You get into bed with her. Lily turns her head away, but she lets you take her in your arms and hold her.

"You asked me about the movies," you say. "Let me tell you about movies. When I got here from Cuba, I learned a lot of English from the movies. I learned to talk like the actors and lose my accent and be an American. That's all it was at first. Later, it was different. Movies became about escape. I imagined that I could step into the screen and become part of the movie and everything would turn out okay. For a long time, it was like being really sick and staying indoors in bed, all the while knowing that other kids were playing outside in the sunshine. Escape was so close. I could almost touch the life I wanted. Freedom was in front of me, if I could just step through that window."

"Why couldn't you be like the other kids?"

You ignore her question. "Movies are what set Americans' dreams so high. Every guy wants to be the best of the guys they see on screen and we all want a woman like you to tell us we've made it. We all want a woman like you, Lily. I want you to say...to be able to say that I pass. I met the movie standard and I'm one of the good ones."

Lily turns to look at you and puts her head on your shoulder. "As long as we're part of this mess, this war, the Machine...as long as Jimmy Lima's alive and as long as my father can find me...you're never going to be that guy, Jesus."

You're quiet for a long time before you tell her you have a plan. "The way out is through."

"Are we free on the other side, Jesus? Is it like we're in a movie and everything works out in the end and we can look each other in the eye when we're done and be sure we're the righteous ones?"

"Somebody once said that life is all about sex, death and mind control. If you can get the first, accept the second and use the third, you can be happy. We could be happy if we exercise a little mind control."

Cars start up and rumble off from the parking lot. You hear a maid vacuuming the room next door. Finally, Lily tells you the thing you have feared most.

"If you want me with you on the other side of that plan," she says, "you're going to have to tell me the truth. All of it. Harv said something about the skim. What's the skim? How did Uncle Bob die?"

"You can be a hard woman, Lily."

"Tell me everything or I walk out that door. I'll go to the cops. I'll get protection from the FBI and you'll never see me again. I'll tell them I killed Harv to protect you and you're mixed up in a gang war that killed two little kids. If you hold anything back, I'll never forgive you and you will never, ever have your movie ending. You'll never have me and I'll never love you and I'll spit on your grave. And, yes, 'spit' is a euphemism. Believe it."

You don't consider your options. You don't even hesitate. You tell Lily everything.

MISSION POSSIBLE

A couple of Vincent's soldiers are watching the emergency entrance and another guy you recognize hangs out by the elevator on Vincent's floor. Hospital security is the easiest security to bypass if you are wearing scrubs and stick to the stairwells. You wear a lab coat over a scrub top with tiny ponies running across it. The only thing that doesn't fit are your black eyes. You still look like a raccoon so you wear big sunglasses. To top off the disguise, you carry a clipboard and wear a stethoscope around your neck. You blend in with some nurses coming in a side door from a smoke break. You're in.

Denny told you stories of mobsters who dressed up as women to whack somebody, but it's hard to imagine most hit men would do it because if things go wrong, you don't want to die wearing pantyhose. You wonder how Denny is now and if they've found the storage locker yet. How much money is the skim, anyway?

The hospital's cleaners try to cover up the smell of fear with industrial bleach. It's an insult to your intelligence, trying to make you forget that this is the place people come to die. In Vincent Lima's case, it's the place to put off dying a little longer. He had to argue to get the prostate surgery. His doctors refused him at first, declaring that at his advanced age, the anaesthesia might kill him before the cancer got the chance. He's a tough old guy, a bullet eater and much loved, if for no other reason than that he has survived this long and he's still in the game.

Behind schedule, you get lost in the rabbit's warren between Radiology and hallways of empty offices that all look alike. You have to wander around, but you finally spot Marv by the entrance to the cafeteria. As soon as he spots you he taps his temple as if he has forgotten something — all systems go — and heads out the far door with you trailing behind. He gets on the elevator. You take the stairs.

Vincent is on the fifth floor. He's supposed to be discharged today around five. It's 4:30. As long as the guys downstairs don't come up to ask if the big boss is ready, you might pull this off without a hitch. It looked good on paper, but everything looks good on paper on the first pass. In the military, they taught you all battle plans are solid until you actually confront the enemy.

As you come to the top step, you see down the hall and spot Paulie Munoz at Vincent's door. Marv stands behind him, looking sharp in a blue pinstriped suit. If not for the *M* on his neck, he could pass for a tall, buff accountant. According to plan, Marv tells Paulie that he's to help out by providing a little extra security for the boss on Jimmy's orders. Given that the Romanians will be out for vengeance as soon as they get over the shock of their loss, that makes a lot of sense.

Paulie's eyes are on Marv, but as soon as Marv sees you coming through the stairwell door at the end of the hall, he gives Paulie the nod. Paulie spins and sees you coming with the clipboard out front.

"Jesus Diaz!" Paulie smiles and waves, a huge toothy grin spreading across his face, but he's reaching for his gun as Marv smacks him behind the ear with the butt of the Smith & Wesson taken from Denny's arsenal. Paulie's legs wobble but he's not out. It's easy to give anyone a concussion, but that doesn't mean they crumple and go to sleep. For that, Marv wraps his arms around Paulie's neck while you pry the gun from his hand.

Paulie's eyes roll back and he's out. Cat taught Marv that chokehold well: under the chin, scoop up, squeeze in and lock down the carotid arteries and it's beddy-bye time. Paulie didn't have a chance with you and Marv coming at him from both sides. In the military, you learned that if you find yourself in a fair fight, you've failed to plan properly.

Marv holds Paulie under the armpits while you grab his legs and carry him to a gurney. A patient, an elderly woman with frizzy hair, pokes her head out of her room. She looks worried. "Should I call a nurse?"

"No worries, ma'am," you say in your best Australian accent. "He doesn't care for the bleach smell. Fainted. You know how it is. Some people have a hard time with hospitals."

She comes out of her room a few more steps tied to an IV pole by the needle and hose in her arm. "Yeah...my dad had that problem. Fainted at the sight of blood."

You turn your back to the old woman and block

her view of Paulie. "We should get the patient into a room, don't you think, doctor?" you tell Marv in your most official voice. You're already pushing a door open with your back and wheeling the gurney into a large room.

A man lying in a bed by the window looks up from reading a book. "Excuse me. This is a private room."

Paulie's coming around so Marv pulls the curtain closed, screening him in so the guy by the window can't see him. Paulie's undoubtedly going to have a huge headache. You zip tie him to the gurney while Marv takes off his tie and stuffs it in Paulie's mouth. Paulie's eyes lock on yours and you hesitate, just for a second, before pulling the pillowcase over his head.

You lean close to Paulie and whisper, "We're here for Vincent. There's a Romanian guy outside the door with a straight razor. He's under orders to cut your throat if you call for help. I'd be really quiet if I were you. That was his little niece and nephew you guys killed. The Romanian won't need much provoking, you know what I mean? "

Paulie nods.

"This is going to be over in a few minutes. Just relax." Paulie nods again.

You've done some jobs with Paulie. He's not a bad guy. He is just doing his job just like you were when Jimmy told you to whack Panama Bob. You do Paulie a favor. "Stay away from Jimmy Lima's house. When you get out of here, go home and have a long nap and put some ice on your head. Lay low. A storm's coming."

You slip out from behind the curtain and the man in the bed still looks pissed. "Excuse me! I told you this is a private room! I paid for a *private* room!"

You pick up his chart from the end of his bed and pretend to study it. You take the pen from the breast pocket of your lab coat, circle something at random and sign your name: Dr. James Bond. "Cutbacks, sir. I'm sorry, sir. You shoulda voted Democrat."

"Wh-whuh?" He looks white, fat and puffy, like just about anybody who can afford a private room.

"The charge for the private room will be deducted from your bill. Please be quiet. If you disturb the other patient with excess noise, his throat might collapse permanently. A nurse and someone from hospital administration will look in on you shortly to sort out your room assignment. We're moving you to a room with a jacuzzi." You return the chart to the end of his bed and turn away. You leave the lab coat and scrubs in the bathroom before you're out the door.

Marv stands at attention outside Vincent's door when you pop into the hall. He doesn't conceal his admiration. "Respect, bro! It's amazing how easy the lying comes to you. You don't hesitate. If I were Lily, as fine as she is — don't get me wrong — I sure wouldn't trust you with all the maids around your mansion you're going to have when we're done with this."

"As a kid, I was trained by experts to think one thing while saying the opposite," you whisper. You're thinking of the words *yes,* and *I love you* and *thank you.* "Plus, I've seen all the *Mission Impossible* movies and watched a lot of improv."

A moment later, you're standing in the old man's hospital room. He sits in a wheelchair, dressed and ready to go with an orange paperback in his lap, facing the door.

Vincent Lima's lined face betrays no emotion, but he says, "Marv! And young Diaz! I didn't expect to see you."

"We gotta go, Boss," Marv says. "The *Banda* is out for revenge for car bombing the Cob."

"After what happened to his children, I don't blame the Romanians. Cob was a good target but getting the kids...that's too bad. Jimmy really screwed the pooch all the way around on this one. Killing kids gets everybody in an uproar. After the funeral of the little boy and girl, they'll come for us."

"We got a tip that they're going to assassinate you here!" Marv says. "We've got to get you back home where we can protect you."

"I was going home today, anyway. I was supposed to talk with the doctors before I left, but I guess they can call me."

"Are you in pain, Boss?" you ask.

"At my age, pain is all I've got and all I can do is to try to give it away and not piss my pants too much. Where's Paulie?"

"Driving the decoy car."

"That's what he's good for. I'll be glad to let you boys give me a ride."

Marv takes point and you push the wheelchair. You're halfway down the hall before Vincent peers back at you and says, "You look pretty good for a dead guy. Jimmy told me you were dead, or as good as."

"Aside from a couple of black eyes and a bad beating, I'm feeling pretty good, sir."

"Sir. Heh. What's the plan? You gonna whack me for the *Banda*? How much are the Romanians paying you? I can top it."

"This isn't about you, sir. But I need to have a talk with Jimmy."

"So you're telling me on your word of honor, on your mother's name, that I'm not going to end up in your trunk today?" He smiles. The old guy has old school style.

"My mother's name was Maritza and I'm not here to kill you, sir."

"Respect."

Marv plows ahead, scanning for Machine security, but there's no resistance along the escape route. You're already out a side door beside Radiology and headed across the back parking lot to the street.

Vincent looks up at the late afternoon sun, closes his eyes and his shoulders loosen. "What do you want to talk to my son about, young Diaz?"

"He ordered me to murder your other son, sir. Bob was skimming, sir. I'm sorry to say it, but it's true. The car bombing wasn't necessary. He killed that Romanian guy and his two kids for nothing. He knocked off Bob so he'd be your only heir to the throne. He wants me dead so no one's around to say otherwise when he takes the whole Machine to war against the *Banda*. Jimmy's gone nuts."

The old man's chin sinks to his chest and you almost miss his mumble. "Some throne. I'm a king of idiots."

Just for a moment, from the side, you think you catch a hint of a grim smile. You should know what's coming next. You aren't driving Vincent Lima to Jimmy's house as a hostage. Vincent's taking you for a ride.

WHAT WILL STOP HIM

Marv sits behind the wheel and revs the engine while you help Vincent Lima into his car. You sit in the back seat of the 1966 four-door, hardtop Cutlass Supreme with the old man. The make and model, also known as the Holiday Sedan, is the same as Vincent's first car when he was coming up. Everything is original except the custom paint job: "It's bright red, for the flag of Navarre, where I was born," Vincent explains. "After the Italian Families blew up my first car in '73 — a misunderstanding — I bought another one just like the original. It's a lucky car and we all need luck."

"So the bomb went off early or something?"

"An old friend of mine, name of Jimenez, was borrowing the original for a date. Good guy. He first brought me into The Machine before I spoke any English at all. Fresh off the boat, as they say. He never made it to the date. That car was lucky for me. Not so lucky for Jimenez. The girl he was going to meet later on became my first wife. Funny, huh?"

"How long before the Italians stopped trying to blow you up?"

"Give up enough money and territory and they can be very reasonable and forgiving. I love the Italians. Good food. There's a shake up every ten years or so, but they understand the Code and they get that we all make more money when we're peaceful. We are kingdoms. We respect the borders of those kingdoms and there's room for everybody. Usually. Sometimes...sometimes it's worth it to shake things up so you get more territory. It's not about the lives it costs in the short-term." Vincent looks at you pointedly. "Good soldiers die for larger causes. Just like with the whole country, it's about the money and the respect."

The old man's smile is full and unforced. He's supposed to be your bargaining chip, but instead, you're the one with fear skittering up your spine like cold spiders. What was it Lily said? *Fear is easy to spot. It's everywhere.*

"You know, Jesus... What old guys like Pete and me understand, 'cause we've been through the worst of things, is *loyalty*. We need guys who know how to follow orders and keep their traps shut. You were in the army. You know. The Machine's a private army that serves a business, just like any other army. In the regular army, no matter who a guy is, he doesn't do what he's supposed to do? Treason. Dead. Simple."

You sit back and nod and cross your arms, your right hand slipping around the grips of your SIG Sauer. You could shoot him right through your jacket and surely Vincent knows it, but he speaks with the confidence of a man who Death has missed on so many occasions, he's sure he can't be killed.

"When I was coming up, younger than you, Diaz, I

found that I had a talent for working things out with people. My old boss? Anbessa. Long before you came along, Anbessa called me The Ambassador. I could make things right. Maybe a few eggs would get broken and there'd be some ketchup in the omelette, but I could do what it took to make things right and make The Machine safe. We respect the Blue so the local cops stay out of our business mostly and we respect the Code...mostly. The threats to The Machine's business are often not from the outside. It's ungrateful people you take in and feed, people who sit across from you at your table in your own home where you cooked the food. The ones closest to you are the ones to watch, Jesus."

"Yes, sir."

"You won't remember this, but some guys got remote car starters when the remotes first came out."

"Denny told me about it. He said he's done some wiring for you over the years."

"Yeah. Well...car starters are a great way for fat, lazy people to get fatter and lazier. Hard to believe the citizens we got now come from the same people who travelled across the world's oceans in sailboats. Most people won't get off the couch now unless it's for candy. But for guys like us? Those remotes sure beat getting your wife to start your car. Trouble was, it caught on too much and the big bosses started looking harder at the guys who bought those car remotes."

Your palm feels wet on the SIG's grip. All this talk of remote starters and car bombs makes you sweat.

"Guys thought they were pretty clever. They said it was to warm up the car, of course, but it doesn't get *that* cold in New York. New York can get chilly, but we're soldiers. We make the city tough and the city makes us tough, am I right? If they thought there was a chance they'd get blown up some morning, they got a car starter installed. Those guys were scared and it started to make us think somebody was definitely up to something. Least that was the word. Then Anbessa — great guy, smart guy even for a wise guy — got suspicious of these three guys with remote car starters. One morning, they got blown up. It was in all the newspapers. The Machine got a little smaller that year, but I moved up faster."

"So you didn't get a remote because it might make your old boss suspicious of you? I thought you wouldn't do it because you didn't want to mess up your classic car with wiring for a remote starter."

"It wasn't quite so classic then. Then it was just old. No, I moved up because *I* was the guy wiring three cars to explode one morning. Three jobs in one night! I never had a remote starter, but I did keep my car locked up in a garage every night, which is what those guys shoulda done, the rats."

"That's why those guys got blown up? They were all rats?"

"Well, I speak too harshly. One of 'em was, for sure, yeah. We heard later that the feds' investigation stalled out after that morning. It's a shame."

You hear his words, but you can't detect any tone that sounds like true regret.

"We never figured out which of the three was the one who wasn't righteous. It's a terrible thing, Jesus, to kill a friend, a fellow soldier, a *brother*." The way Vincent looks at you, you know he knows about Rodolpho and the red churning water beyond the propeller blades. The only person you ever told about

Rodolpho was the kid you adopted as your new brother. Vincent has had long talks about you with Denny, you're sure.

"Yes," you say finally. "Yes, it *is* a terrible thing to lose a brother."

"But you gotta do what you gotta do to save The Machine. In Viet Nam, they said we bombed the village to save the village. Sacrifices are made so we get to keep what we fought for. Sometimes terrible sacrifices. Sometimes, you even have to kill a son to save a family."

Marv pushes the button on the visor to activate the first gate to Jimmy Lima's place. He turns the wheel and you're through and on your way up the long drive to The Castle. Denny will be there with the key. Or maybe they figured out where to find the storage locker and already picked up Panama Bob's skim. All that doesn't matter anymore. Vincent sees your game and he is ice.

We all need luck, he said. Your luck drains away, flushing your life with it.

"You sleep okay, Jesus? I sleep okay. My own prostate swoll up and tried to kill me, but I still sleep okay. You know the secret?"

"Sir?"

"The secret to success and dealing with all of life's troubles and sleeping fine and letting go of worry and stress…. Everything civilians don't get but we have to learn if we're going to be soldiers and make ourselves useful cogs in The Machine? You know that secret to overcoming all of life's difficulties?"

"What's the secret to all that, sir?"

"Not minding. Not minding, doing what you gotta do. But you, my young friend? I think you've learned this lesson too late.”

He knows you've got your hand on your SIG, yet he doesn't look the least bit worried. Now you know what Vincent won't do and what will stop him: Nothing.

You *do* mind. You should worry, so you do, all the way up the long driveway to Jimmy Lima's castle in Great Neck. The end is coming fast.

DESCENT

Bald Van is on the inner gate, strutting back and forth with his heavy combat shotgun, a SPAS-12. Van has told you on many occasions it's the same model used in the video games he loves. The SPAS-12 in Van's hands is a very dangerous thing. Unlike most of Vincent's guys, Van spends time practicing with his weapons at a range. All mob guys carry, but few can be bothered to put in enough time to know how to put bullets in the right places.

Back in Denny's apartment, Marv tried to convince you a night attack on Jimmy's castle would be the smart way to go. You told him going ninja was the quick way to breaking an ankle jumping down from the high wall that surrounds Jimmy's place. The grounds are patrolled by dogs at night and getting your throat ripped out is a hard way to go. The closer you get to the big house, despite your muscle and your surprises and an old man for a hostage, now you wish you'd taken your chances with the guard dogs' teeth.

Marv slows the Cutlass for a moment so Van can see Vincent sitting beside you in the back. As soon as he sees him, Van signals Chico to open the gate. Chico carries a bolt-action Remington Model 700 sniper rifle with a long can — a noise suppressor screwed into the end of the long gun's muzzle — and he quickly steps up to slide the heavy iron gate back on its wheels. Chico's weapon has a bipod folded under the barrel for stability and accuracy on the long shots. It's a standard issue police rifle used for containment, but it's a slow, stupid choice for a sentry on a gate. Assuming you get to live long enough to fight your way out past this dunce, it's not a good time to tell him he should be making smarter hardware choices.

As the Cutlass slides up the driveway, you spot Freejack Jack. He's out on the front lawn in cutoffs tossing a disc back and forth with a pretty girl in a barely-there-in-the-right-spots tankini.

Twist and Juan, each carrying Uzis, run out and herd Jack and his squeeze toward the guesthouse by the pool in back of the mansion. You look through the back window and catch a glimpse of Chico talking into a walkie-talkie. Jimmy already knows you're here with his father. There doesn't seem to be any other muscle around, though, so Jimmy's not worried about you and he must not expect trouble from the Romanians until after the funeral for Boss Cob and his kids.

Twist and Juan stick too close together as they follow Freejack Jack and the tankini girl. That might come in handy. Twist and Juan are best friends, but they joke around too much while on duty and stand too close together to be smart. A single spray of bullets, or a nearby explosion, could take them both out at once.

Freejack disappears out of sight around the corner of the mansion, safely out of the line of fire. When Jimmy brought Freejack Jack in, he was way outside the world of The Machine. He went to college and made no bones. He's a computer guy and the accountant. Every gang has some guys who are good at math, but he just wasn't street enough for the job. Before he moved into the guesthouse and girls started showing up, Denny told you he was sure the guy was a twink.

"No man wears cutoff jeans that short, dawg," Denny said. "I'm telling you, Jimmy wants a little strange nearby, but it's not pussy he's looking for. It's some guy's mouth-pussy."

You shrugged and had nothing to say. "Jimmy's business."

"Jimmy's done time, man," Denny persisted. "You know how that goes. Some guys go to jail and they're gay for the stay. Sometimes when they get out, they still can't pray the gay away."

When Cat Fornes got hired, Denny started speculating about Jimmy's love life again. The cage fighter's muscles were huge, but his masculine image was softened by his high voice and his lisp. Big Denny was sure Jimmy Lima was banging his bodyguard instead of Barbara. Looking back, maybe it was then that Big Denny decided to risk his life and move in on Barbara.

You didn't care then, but now you wonder if Cat Fornes got Bob's skim and took off and that's why no one's seen him. Maybe you're risking everything for nothing and you should just be running with what little cash you have on hand. If you had the courage to leave Lily drunk and asleep in that Jersey motel, you could be a bus driver in California in a month.

Maybe the skim is what Hitchcock called a MacGuffin: The one thing everybody in the movie is after but either nobody gets it or it doesn't really matter, anyway. In *Pulp Fiction*, the MacGuffin was just something shiny and valuable in a case, but Tarantino let you squirm and speculate what it might be as the body count climbed higher.

Then you think about Lily crying into your chest, looking for an out, God's blessing, forgiveness or at least escape. You think about all her talk about free will versus fate. To you, the skim is no MacGuffin. The skim matters plenty because you've got to get out of The Machine, stop being a cog and get away. You want a chance at having choices. The farther you roll up the driveway and the closer you get to the key, the less likely it seems you'll make it back down this driveway.

You've visited Jimmy's house many times, but your palms have never sweated like this. Marv wheels the big Cutlass around the fountain in the circular driveway and parks at the front door. Jimmy Lima trots down the stairs with a bandage on his neck. When Marv steps out from the driver's seat, Jimmy gives him a nod and you can't see any change in his expression. Has Marv turned on you? Jimmy only slows half a step when he spots you beside his father.

He freezes when he sees your arms are crossed with your hand under your suit jacket, but before you can speak up, Vincent takes charge for you. "Young Diaz would like to have a talk, so I think we should call a meeting, Jimmy. We can clear the air. How's the neck?"

Of course Jimmy already told the boss that you stabbed him in the neck with a fork.

"It's fine, Pop." He rubs his neck, nonetheless. If he could set you on fire by sheer force of will, you'd already be screaming.

You had hoped Jimmy would keep his father out of the loop as long as he was in the hospital, but that was too much to hope for. It's not just that Vincent wasn't flustered when you showed up. He must have *expected* you.

He's right. The trick is not minding and Vincent has that knack. You've got Marv on your side and a couple of surprises to come, but despite the SIG in your hand, Vincent is still the man driving this bus.

You get out on your side, closer to the house, your hand still under your jacket, as Marv helps Vincent out of the car on the other side.

"Where's Paulie?" Jimmy asks.

Vincent leans on the Cutlass's trunk for support and barks out a laugh. "These guys took him out easy. I didn't hear a thing. My hearing's not so good anymore, but still, very pro. I didn't know for sure he had me until he walked in my hospital room. Very smooth. Jesus, you'll be a real loss to the organization."

You ignore the compliment and the threat. "Paulie's alive and tied to a gurney. He probably still thinks there's a Romanian on the door waiting for an excuse to cut him up."

Jimmy points at Marv. "You turning your back on us, too, Marvin? You throw in with the little Cuban? What? Did he tell you a story and you believed him? You should never believe a word from this guy."

"This isn't about you or Jesus, Jimmy. This is

about *family*. Jake killed my brother. I know he's here. You know what I've got to do." To everyone's surprise, Marv is crying. He pulls out the Smith & Wesson ahead of schedule. He doesn't point the pistol at anyone — it's down by his side in a listless hand. "Give me Jake Cibrian so I can avenge my brother and I'm done."

You don't have time to shout a warning or get the situation back under control. Jimmy's still pointing at Marv, two fingers out and thumb up like he's a kid pretending he's holding a pistol.

"You're already done," Jimmy says. He raises his other hand to his ear and tugs the lobe. Marv's head explodes with a very precise one-shot kill from a . 308 round.

You underestimated Chico. He must be putting time in at the range with Van. You throw yourself to the ground behind the Cutlass before Chico can chamber the next round. Your gun is out but Jimmy stomps on your arm. You might have kicked out and taken Jimmy down with you, but there's Bald Van with the SPAS-12's muzzle digging into your back. You never saw Bald Van coming. You were focused on the wrong details, watching faces instead of watching your back. You drop the SIG.

You walked in with an old man for a hostage and Marv for muscle — a guy you conned into being an ally. Now you have nothing.

Almost nothing.

You still have hope until Van tells you to get up. At the top of the stairs stands a big man with cold eyes. Big Denny De Molina, the friend and adopted brother you killed. It's hard to imagine you ever worried about having to kill him again. He's on crutches with one leg in a plaster cast that reaches from his right ankle to his crotch. His lower lip trembles and you take in at a glance that when you nearly killed him, you hurt him in ways no cast can heal. But that's not the crazy part.

Big Denny is flanked by two beautiful women. One is Jimmy's wife, Barbara. She is the woman Big Denny loves so much, he tried to kill you to protect their secret. But that's not the craziest part.

The other woman is the only woman on earth you'd kill for. Lily is dressed entirely in red, down to her three-inch, come-hump-me pumps. But you're the one who's really fucked, aren't you? In the next few minutes, before you're murdered, it might be nice to figure out if Lily is the one woman on the planet worth dying for. That's pretty far out there, but still not the craziest part.

"Take it easy, Jesus," Lily says. "I talked to Daddy and Papa Vincent. They have a plan. We're all going to get out of this alive as long as you don't do anything stupid." Lily says that like she believes it. That's the craziest part.

YOU'VE COME UNDONE

Pete and Jake are waiting in the great room. In most houses, this would be called the living room, but not in a castle like Jimmy's. From the front window, beyond Vincent's Cutlass and the fountain, the vast front lawn — the "grounds" when they're this big — stretch out to the inner gate. It's a long way to run and, assuming you can get out of here, Chico will have a few shots at you before you cross the lawn. You probably won't even make it as far as the fountain.

Bald Van is thorough. He takes your trench coat and removes your chain and hockey stick tool. He takes the knife from your sock and, careful not to scratch the white wood, places it delicately on the Baby Grand piano beside your SIG Sauer P220 and the extra mags . You've eaten with these guys, played pool and poker with them and worked beside them. They know your usual weapons and where you keep them.

Van leans on the wall by the window but keeps his gaze fixed on you. He flicks the shotgun muzzle an inch and waggles his eyebrows and you take a seat.

Big Denny lowers his bulk to the loveseat awkwardly, his broken leg straight out. Pete and Jake sit on a sectional couch and glare at you. Jimmy and Lily sit behind you along the back wall. Vincent sits across from you so he can look into your eyes.

"You've forced my hand, Jesus," Vincent begins. "I'm going to have to air the family's dirty laundry, though maybe that's for the best anyway. Baldy, you sweep this room? No bugs?"

Van nods.

"For sure?"

"Swept for insects twice, sir. The Feds don't have a prayer."

"Fine."

Pete trembles as he stares at you. His fists are clenched. "What were you thinking bringing my daughter into this?"

If they're going to kill you anyway, you may as well go out with style. "She likes black eyes."

"What?"

"Denny gave me black eyes and Lily found me irresistible. I understand your confusion. At first, I thought she meant that she liked black guys."

Jake guffaws but Pete silences him with a hard look. Vincent at least has the grace to smile. From behind you, Lily whispers for you to shut up.

"Yeah, better you shut up, Jesus," Vincent says good-naturedly. "This is the point in your story where all the interested parties gather and things get explained, just like in an old Nero Wolfe detective story. Only you're no detective. You think you're smart, but you're not so smart. You're the guy things happen to. I'm the guy who makes things happen. Understand?"

"So far I do. Speak slow."

"You punk!" Pete rises and steps close, drawing back his hand. He hasn't taken his ring off. You imagine that ring will hurt when it connects and you wince and turn your head, hoping to roll with the expected blow. The strike never comes. When you open your eyes, Lily stands between you and her father. She says nothing. She just shakes her head and Pete lowers his hand.

"Everybody have a seat," Vincent says. "I'm going to break this down for you. There are complications coming our way because of a lack of discipline and loyalty in the ranks. This, I will not tolerate. You don't get a house like this, Jimmy, by being sloppy. You especially don't continue to keep it if you're going to be sloppy. We've gotten weak and lazy. If we're going to grow, we need to toughen up and clear out the dead wood. With discipline, we could be so much bigger than we are. For the rest of The Machine to work better, we've got to make examples of those who would fail us. Harsh discipline builds a legacy. Remember this: I am not the bad guy here. I'm the fucking king. I make the tough decisions today to make sure there's a castle here tomorrow."

Vincent turns to Pete. "Speaking of things that make me sad, the kid played you with an old scam and that's one thing that's got you pissed. The second thing that's got you pissed is that your only daughter is still hanging out with this loser."

Vincent turns to you. "Pete came to me months ago and asked me for permission to whack you, Jesus. I said no. I told him the little guy could be useful and if there's a shit job that comes up that could get him killed, then maybe I'd use you. I also told him that Lily is a beautiful young woman and she should make her own choices...up to a point. Let them date and be young and feel their wild oats and later, Lily will settle down with someone of substance."

Lily crosses her arms and looks sour.

"Don't even," Pete says. "This is not the place or the time for you to be the rebellious kid. I'm sorry, Vincent. I spoiled her."

Vincent turns to Pete and shakes his head. "That's not what you should be apologizing for, Pete. Jake tells me that as soon as you fell for Jesus's grift — magically making counterfeit money out of real bills — you were plotting against Jimmy and telling yourself it was for me and The Machine's own good. Think about it a minute longer and it's clear you were thinking of promoting yourself."

Pete glares at Jake, but before he can move, Jake stands up, pulls his pistol and levels it at Pete's midsection. Pete sits back on the couch, his mouth a thin line, while Jake reaches into Pete's jacket and removes his pistol and sticks it in his own belt.

"You thought you saw an opening," Vincent says. "You thought I was weak. I'm old. You, of all people, should know the difference between old and weak, Pete."

"Dad, can't we deal with this somewhere else?" Jimmy says. "I don't want this to happen in my own home. Marv's corpse is bleeding on my front step, for Christ's sake!"

"Shut up, Jimmy. I'll get to you in a minute. Ordinarily, I'd agree. But we're all here and I just had prostate surgery, so you'll excuse me if I'm not up for any more travel and shenanigans today. Where were we?"

"You just made Pete aware that I'm going to be buried with him," you say in a cheerful, helpful tone.

"Pete's an old friend. I'm not going to let Jake shoot him in front of Lily. Lily's like a granddaughter to me. It's not that kind of day. But Pete? You disappoint me. Deep. Jimmy's the heir apparent, but you would have still been his chief adviser when I give up the ghost. That's not going to happen now. You're demoted. You get to keep your book, but I'm going to need to take ten percent more starting now. Also, the after-hours club is all mine. Any questions?"

Pete looks at the carpet and shakes his head.

"I didn't fucking think so," the old man says genially. "Jake, put the heater away. You look a little too eager to use it. You were loyal, so you'll be working with me from now on. Paulie's a good guy, but obviously too stupid since instead of being here he's tied to a hospital bed. You're my new driver, Jake. Congrats."

"I just want to pipe up here, sir," you point out, "Lily doesn't want to see *me* killed in front of her, either. And you should know I'm a bleeder, Jimmy. I'm really going to mess up this fine carpet."

"We'll use a plastic bag, then," Big Denny says.

A plastic bag. That cold bastard. You wish you'd never told Denny the truth about your history in that terrible basement in Florida. You wish you'd never saved him. You wish lots of things. Except for getting Lily, your wishes have never come true. Now that's slipping away, too.

Vincent ignores Denny. He's back to watching your eyes so you stare back. All the lies are out. All you can do is own them and wait for your moment. Your moment better come quickly, before Denny steps behind you and slips a plastic bag over your head and seals it off with a zip tie around your throat.

Vincent shifts uncomfortably in his seat and takes a pill bottle from his jacket, opens it, and knocks back a couple oblong tablets, swallowing the painkillers dry. "You think just because I went under the knife that *now's* your opening? I'll give up The Machine when I choose. I didn't work my way up for so long to have one of you apes just step in the moment I hit a speed bump. I'm bigger than cancer, boys. I've dodged bullets for years. I sure as shit can deal with you humps. Get it?"

The men nod. You allow a shrug. You consider telling Vincent that you just wanted the skim so you could get out and far away. You didn't have any designs on a quick promotion. The old man doesn't look so genial anymore, so you shut up.

"Next, just so you all understand once and forever that I am not weak, *I* gave the order for Bob to get whacked. "

The blood drains from your face. You can feel it.

"I told Jimmy to order Jesus to whack Bobby. It tore my heart out to do it. My own step son. I never thought of him like that. I always, always just called Bobby my son. But he got greedy. I could even stand that. I understand that. There's too thin a line between ambition and greed. Under the right circumstances, Bob might even have been a good boss someday. But he had his gambling problem. I can't abide weakness. Stupid, I'm used to. Weakness, I can't stand. But worse, Bob was talking to the feds."

Mouths drop open around the room. Even Bald Van, who you thought wasn't listening, looks more pale. He leans back against the window pane, cooling the back of his head.

"So..." you venture, "this was never about the skim."

"Nope. I could tolerate a little of that. I gave him rope. I knew about his gambling debts in Atlantic City. I wanted him to grow up and deal with it himself. If I had stepped in earlier, maybe the feds wouldn't have gotten their hooks into him so deep. They picked him up with a limo outside a casino in Atlantic City and gave him a dream of escape from us, after we gave him so much."

"How did you know for sure?" you ask, thinking of how Vincent car bombed three guys, knowing only one of them was the rat.

Vincent shrugs. "There's lots more going on behind the scenes than you imagine, kid. Like all little guys, you think the game is all about you. You're the worst kind of dummy. You're the kind of dummy who thinks he's smart. You think all I do is sit back and drink wine while you run your little errands and it's your world. Meanwhile? I'm a business man. I cultivate people. I have meetings. One day I get a phone call from an FBI agent. He tells me I've got a rat and for an exorbitant amount of money, he'll show me proof who it is. I met with this bastard, heard a tape and saw some photos and I was still crying when I paid that FBI bastard his money for the information. I would have excommunicated Bob and left it at that if it weren't for the feds. Bob threatened the entire Machine. Bob wanted out, but he wanted us to fund his retirement and then live high off the hog in some WitSec program. A fat guy like Bob, he wasn't going to testify and let the feds ship him off to be a shoe salesman in Arizona with a new name. He wanted to get out, to send us all to jail where we wouldn't chase after him and keep the skim, too."

"My brother was a rat?" Jimmy looks ashen.

"Easy, Jimmy. When I told you to have the little Cuban whack Bob, you didn't fight me so hard. You thought this was just about the skim. You couldn't have loved Bob that much. You're not so different from Pete, here. You saw your ascent in Bob's fall."

"You told me to give Jesus the job. I don't question your orders, Dad."

"Sh. *Sh!* Don't pretend it was loyalty. Sure, there's that, but it was self-interest more. That's the problem. We aren't a machine until you get that we are bigger than you. The Machine is bigger than any one of your little dreams. Which brings us to you, little man."

"I'd like to point out that I'm almost 5'9"," you say.

"Good for you. Your legs reach all the way to the ground. Your problem is you got your head in the clouds. Diaz, Lily tells me you want out of The Machine, too. You saw the skim as a way out. You wanted to take Bob's skim and whirl our little Lily far away from all that we've given her."

"Would you have let me go if I'd come to you?"

Vincent laughs. "You were in the army. Did they just let you go when you asked to go home?"

You shrug. "I got out. At first I thought all I had to do was kiss a sergeant. Turns out that doesn't work with all sergeants. Some, you have to break their jaws."

"You're a funny guy, Jesus."

"You say that like pretty girls say they like a guy with a sense of humor. Then they end up dating some prick with money whose jokes are lame."

"Why am I here for this?" Lily says. "You said it was going to be all right. You said I could be in the room. I thought if I was in the room, that meant you were serious that everything was going to be okay. You'd give us the key to the storage locker and your blessing and we'd walk out of here. You promised me everything would be all right, *Abuelo*!"

"Shut up, kiddo. I'm not your *abuelo*. Since Pete has proved himself disloyal, sadly, I'm now simply your father's pissed off employer. I said everything would be all right. I didn't say *how*. I got a machine to oil if we're all going to stay out of federal prison, so you just shut up. You aren't hearing me. You're too pretty for your own good, Lily. Always were. We have always spoiled you and this is our reward. You think everything is just about you, too. You think the money for your car, your apartment, your education...that it all falls from the sky and you stay clean? Nobody's clean. Everybody has a dirty hand in."

Lily steps back and leans her hip against your shoulder. It's a silent apology that's way too late. Moving slowly so Bald Van won't blow your head off, you offer her your hand and she takes it.

Vincent sighs. "Young love. The most stupid love of all. Lily, you got the curves but you don't have the brains. You don't understand what it takes to do what we have to do. I had my own son killed. What makes you think you're so special?"

Lily looks up and with a defiant sneer you know

too well says, "I killed Harv with a frying pan."

Vincent didn't know that. You can see it in his face. Jake must have told him *you* killed Marv's twin.

Pete leans forward, his head in his hands. "What am I going to tell your mother? Oh, God...."

"Shut up!" Vincent yells for the first time.

Jimmy smacks you in the back of the head as he steps in from behind your chair. "What the hell is wrong with you? How could you let Lily get in this deep? I thought you said you loved her?"

"She killed Harv with a frying pan because she loved me," you reply. "The rot in The Machine is deeper than you think, Jimmy. Lots of us want out. As soon as Marv and Harv heard about the skim, they were both ready to kill for it to get out and away. Harv was going to kill me to get the key and Lily loves me so much, she killed for me."

Lily squeezes your hand and you feel her warmth flow back into you. The ice in your stomach goes away and you feel more strength. "Marv was going to kill me, but then he thought Jake killed his brother and all he wanted was to get revenge and get out with the skim, too."

"Who told him *I* killed Harv?" Jake asks, bewildered.

"Oh, who do you think, fuckface?" Jimmy says. He fishes out the locker key from his pocket. "Take a good look, Jesus. This is the closest you'll ever get to Panama Bob's skim and the cozy little life you've been plotting with Lily. Millions of women in New York City and you gotta... It's just not done! If Lily weren't the headstrong little princess we all allowed her to be, if anybody in this goddamn room asked permission —"

"Marv was really gonna kill me?" Jake looks at you with new hate in his eyes, but that's okay. He was pretty much full up with hate for you, anyway.

You manage to smile back at him. "It's human nature, Jake. Nobody likes you. And everybody dreams of escaping their regular job, winning the lottery and getting away where there's no boss and we can all live the lives we see in movies. The end part. The happily ever after. We've all got that in us. We've all been sold happily ever after but that's just for movies, I guess."

Vincent's eyes narrow. "And Denny? He rearranged your face pretty good, so can I trust him, or is he a happily ever after guy, too? Was Denny going to kill you for the key, grab the skim and get away from us? Who can I trust, Jesus? If you speak the truth, I'll know. I need to know."

You nod toward Jake. "You can trust him, but he's a moron." You tilt your head toward Bald Van at the window. "You can trust him and he's no idiot, but in a few minutes, he won't be part of the equation."

Vincent's forehead furrows, but before he can interject, your gaze falls on your old friend on the couch, the brother you chose. "Of all of us, Denny's motives were the most pure. Denny didn't care about the skim. He was just trying to get me out of the way to make sure I wouldn't tell anybody his secret. I wish he could have trusted me with the secret. If he had, none of us would be in this mess now and maybe me and Lily would already be living our happily ever after."

Harv and Marv and Panama Bob won't stir up any great sadness in you. You'd planned to kill Marv before this was done, anyway. But the innocent civilian? Denny's neighbor? She didn't have to die. You don't know her name, but you'll never be able to forget her bloody head and her dead eyes staring back at you with accusation.

"What's Big Denny's big secret, Jesus?" Vincent asks. "Convince me. It's time I cleaned The Machine and got it working right. No machine can work right if it's got too many complex parts. Help me clean The Machine and I promise you this: You'll die easy."

"Denny's a loyal cog in The Machine," you say evenly. "He didn't try to kill me for the skim. He tried to kill me so I wouldn't tell anybody that he's in love with Jimmy's wife."

You should expect the punch, but it comes quicker than you can think. Jimmy drives his fist into the side of your face. Maybe you hear a crunch, you're not sure. Certainly, your left eye is going to stay blackened for a long time with all this ongoing abuse. It would if you lived that long, anyway.

Jimmy starts screaming for Barbara but it's Denny he wheels on next. He runs at Denny, who doesn't move from his place on the loveseat. Jimmy's almost on him when Denny lifts one of his crutches and drives the point into Jimmy's solar plexus. Jimmy goes down, clutching his stomach and gasping for air.

Barbara heard Jimmy scream her name and comes running. She stands over him, watching her husband writhe on the floor. He can't talk yet, but he reaches out, his palm up, pleading with his eyes as he struggles for breath.

Barbara doesn't rush to her husband's side. Instead she watches him flop around like a fish on a dock. Her little smile proves that sometimes you do tell the truth.

Jimmy's open palm closes and he points at Barbara. His fingers make a gun. Jimmy's getting his breath back and he uses it to scream. "Kill her! Kill Denny! Kill them both! Do Jesus, too! Do them all! Clean house! Clean house!"

Jake pulls his pistol out again, pointing it first at Denny, then at Barbara. Vincent struggles to stand. It pains him, but he's shouting at Jake, "Don't shoot! Don't shoot! Not here! Not *here*! Not *yet*! No!"

You want to get up in front of Lily, for the little good that will do, but Bald Van trains the SPAS-12 on you and shakes his head.

Pete leaps up from the couch to lunge at Jake. Jimmy shoots him in the shoulder before the bookie can take another step. Pete cries out and spins to the floor, holding his shoulder.

"*Papi!*" Lily screams.

The wound doesn't look bad from where you sit, but everybody knows that once you commit to shooting somebody, you empty that mag so they can never get up and come after you.

Jake's committed to the craziness of the moment now. He draws a bead on Barbara. He's only listening to Jimmy's screams, blocking out everyone else. Jake must have never imagined he'd be ordered to whack the boss's wife. He hesitates and in that moment, Barbara looks her would-be killer in the eyes and crosses the floor to sit on the loveseat beside Denny. She wraps her arms around him and the big lug kisses her. It's the most romantic fucking thing you've ever seen. You could never have dreamed the most romantic gesture you've witnessed in your life would involve Big Denny De Molina.

Lily has slipped behind you by the bookcase full of fake books, her eyes on Jake, screaming to be spared and pleading for her father who writhes on the floor.

"Kill them both, goddammit! Do it!" Jimmy bawls, struggling to his feet.

Jake takes another breath to brace himself for what he's about to do. Barbara and Denny are about to die. The SPAS-12 booms. Jake leaves a bloody smear on the wall as he slides to the floor out of sight behind the big couch.

Your eyes are on the key. *Happily ever after*. It's there, embodied in the little key on the floor at your feet where Jimmy dropped it. Sure, they'll find you wherever you go — earth's not that big — but you could at least escape with Lily for a little while. Ever after isn't in your cards, but escaping for a little while is better than a lot of people ever experience.

However, your prospects to survive the minute are poor. *"Not here, not yet,"* Vincent had said, but soon, obviously. Vincent has the key and now he knows how deep the rot goes. You've got nothing left to give him besides the location of the locker, but since you figured it out, surely Vincent has figured it out, too. Vincent doesn't need you. He'll kill you. He'll clean house just to make sure no one questions that he's still the alpha dog and he's smarter than everybody.

No doubt Vincent is smarter than you on the fly, but you did have some time to prepare. You glance at your watch. The Romanians are late.

TAKE IT

Crash! The Romanians hit the outer gate.

The great room's floor-to-ceiling windows provide an excellent view of the battlefield. The crash is eighty yards away, but the commotion inside the house ends as everyone swivels to look out to see Doom hauling ass up the driveway. A big armoured cube truck — a United States Post Office vehicle — hits the gate and the sheet of iron bars bursts almost all the way inward.

Figures. An armoured truck used by banks is a tough get, but the armoured postal trucks sit in rows beside the regular delivery vehicles, waiting to be stolen. The outer gate is heavier than the driver expected and the truck has to back up and take another run at it before he crashes through. Had the driver committed to hitting the gate at full speed, the element of surprise wouldn't already be slipping away. Two cars following the truck too closely have to wheel out of the way, their tires screeching and smoking to make room for the second run at the iron obstacle.

"It's a bunch of white guys!" Bald Van yells.

"It's the *Banda,*" Vincent says.

An alarm starts up that sounds like a submarine klaxon. From the first floor, running feet pound through the house and, below, Juan and Twist come into view as they run down the front steps. They deke around the Cutlass's back bumper and kneel behind the fountain in the center of the circular driveway. That should be decent cover for them to pick off the Romanians as they pour out of their cars.

Jimmy forgets his adulterous wife and stares out the window in shock. "We got defenses that will make these bitches shit kittens." Even as he says it, five more guards carrying heavy ordnance — four AKs and one guy with a Rocket Propelled Grenade — run out the front of the house to join Juan and Twist. Three kneel in defensive positions behind the fountain. Another squats behind the Cutlass's trunk and the guy with the RPG takes cover behind the car's engine block and shoulders his weapon.

The truck's engine roars, using power rather than speed to slowly push through the steel of the first gate's moorings. It plows a path on to the estate with two cars tight behind, bumper to bumper to bumper. Cracks of gunfire begin. The guys in the back of the second car lean out of their windows to fire at the house. Vincent steps back from the windows.

"Never mind, Dad. The windows are bulletproof," Jimmy says.

"No such thing as bulletproof," Vincent says. "You don't know what they've got in the back of that mail truck."

"We can handle this. Get to the panic room till this blows over. I built this house like a fortress. We don't call it the castle for nothing."

The Boss looks at you. "Is this supposed to be the cavalry coming over the hill for you?"

"We had a talk," you admit. "The Romanians are very angry and vengeance drives a postal truck."

The old man is still ice. He smirks and shrugs. "So you don't just want out, after all. You're a fucking traitor to The Machine, out to destroy us."

"I'm the slipped gear."

Vincent ignores you. "C'mon, Pete. We got a safe spot while the boys take care of business. Barbara? Lily? This isn't your world. Let's go. You've got to be a young idiot with too much testosterone and too many bullets to stay out here and deal with this shit."

The boss has a right to look untroubled. That RPG will tear the vehicles into metal shards, charred flesh and bits of bone. The guys with the Kalashnikovs will clean up the *Banda* before they get anywhere near the front door.

The guys behind the fountain wisely hold their fire, waiting for closer, more realistic targets. However, from behind the inner gate, Chico does a very macho, idiotic thing he probably learned from movies. He stands behind the gate's bars and levels the big Remington at the truck. You can't hear the rifle with that big can on it, suppressing the report, but you see Chico rock from the rifle's kick. He looks like a kid with an air rifle plinking at a tin can with a bb gun.

There's enough space between the outer and inner gates that, this time, the van gets some speed up before it hits the second gate. You're sure Chico will get chewed up under the big truck's wheels in an ugly death, but you're wrong. Nervous and fooling with the rifle bolt too long, he has just enough time to take one step toward safety when the mail truck hits the second gate. When it busts in, the wall of metal sweeps him away like it's a giant's open hand. Everyone stands still, transfixed, as Chico is thrown aside, his body and brains shattered against the wall of the gatehouse. Marv is avenged in a grisly fashion.

"*Ooh!* I thought they'd wait until after the kids' funerals, at least," Jimmy says absently.

"I was sure they weren't going to hit us till at least tonight, after dark." Vincent sounds like a general, surveying a battle, safe behind the front lines. Or so he thinks.

Time to pipe up. "The *Banda* had some inside information, Mr. Lima."

"Shut up!" Jimmy can't look away from the battle. One of his guys opens up. The AK fire is close, but the gunfire is outgoing, not incoming. "This is already over. We can hold off a hundred guys with half a dozen."

You rise from your chair and Bald Van wheels from the window's distractions, the SPAS-12 up and ready to send you bleeding and flying, just like Jake Cibrian. You can't take your eyes off the shotgun's muzzle. Its darkness looks like the future.

"Run Lily! Get out of here! The Romanians are coming. They want vengeance for their boss and his little kids and they're going to get it. Vincent, in a moment, you're going to wonder if murdering a rat son and oiling your machine was worth it. I know you don't care about the money because you've already got plenty. You care if *we* care about the money. You wanted to know who would stay and who would go if they had a chance at a blank slate. Surprise! Anybody with imagination wants out. The

Italians have it right. At least they call their mobs 'families.' You call us your Machine. We ain't cogs and gears. We want to make choices, too. We want to be free."

Vincent looks at Bald Van. "Christ, Van. He's making speeches like fucking Castro over there. Why haven't you blown that little motherfucker's head off, yet?"

The Boss is on the move. It's time.

Bald Van shrugs and raises the shotgun.

"Uh-uh-uh!" You raise one fist high above your head and, perplexed, Van lowers the muzzle a few inches, trying to decipher your play.

"Vincent, you should know that not all the parts on your precious Cutlass Supreme are original anymore."

You open your hand to reveal your keys. On the key ring is a bright red car remote that has big googly eyes and a cartoony smile glued to it. Denny bought the novelty car remote from the same street vendor who sold him the disposable camera on that sunny summer day you took Lily to Coney Island. Denny recognizes it from his own arsenal. With his good leg he kicks, throwing all his weight backward and tipping the loveseat over backward, taking Barbara over with him.

Vincent processes what you said about his car and has just enough time to let his jaw drop slack. Jimmy, oblivious to the real danger, turns only half a step from the window. Bald Van raises the SPAS-12 and tightens up, ready to blow you apart as you throw yourself backward and cover your head with your arms as the shotgun booms. The buckshot cuts the air over your head.

You press the remote's button. The receiver in the Cutlass's trunk detonates the Semtex.

A bright, white flash. BOOM!

You feel the thud of the bomb's concussion through your body as the floor shakes under you. The roar deafens. Your eardrums whine in shock at the concussion.

The remote in Denny's freezer gave you the idea for this frontal assault in daylight. Denny had a brick of C-4 stashed in there, but it was the Romanians who helped you and Marv pack the trunk and wheel wells with Semtex.

The Romanians knew Vincent's car, of course. If you and Marv hadn't driven straight to the *Banda* with the Cutlass, they surely would have shot you in the head when you showed up at their headquarters. When you offered them vengeance for their boss and his two dead children, they didn't smile. They nodded grimly and got to work. You weren't really sure the Romanian electrician who wired the car bomb had done a satisfactory job until the bomb's blast rocked the mansion.

Time warps and you don't know how fast or slow it's passing as the Earth's turning gears of time pause and hitch. Eventually, after who knows how long, you shake your head and roll on to your back. You spot the Baby Grand tipped on one side and roll toward it. You're screaming for Lily, but your voice sounds muffled and far away. You can't find your SIG.

When you chance a peek over the piano, you find that the outdoors is now indoors. Something's on fire and white smoke rolls over you, getting thicker by the minute. The mansion's stone facade has melted away and much of the second floor is gone.

A huge shape with four legs looms haltingly out of the smoke. It's Big Denny De Molina, covered in ash except where his bleeding wounds trickle down the side of his head. His left shoulder sports a deep gash, too. He looks like an angry ghost on crutches. He's got your pistol in his fist. That's it. You're dead. Goodbye Jesus Salvador Umberto Luis Diaz.

You wonder what happens next. When you open your eyes, will you be in Hell? Is it like the priests say? Everlasting pain and flame that burns but never consumes? Will Denny's dead neighbor look down on you from heaven and piss on you from fluffy white clouds, laughing at your pain? Or will Hell mean you're trapped again in the Bug Man's basement, this time forever? Will Tia Marta be a devil holding a plastic bag in one claw and a burning whip in the other? Will all the scars on your back open and never close?

Or will nothing come next? Is Death just darkness and nothingness, a return to the blissful unconsciousness of whatever you were before you were born? That wouldn't be so bad, except there will be no Lily. Lily makes you want to live.

When you open your eyes, Big Denny is leaning on his crutches and Barbara stands by her man. The way Barbara looks at Denny, they're like teenagers who have just shared their last first kiss. You wish Lily looked at you that way, but maybe you've still got a chance at becoming the man who is worthy of that look. Denny grips the SIG by the barrel and holds your weapon out to you. "The pussy's out of the bag now, man. No point killing you now."

You take your pistol and, when helps you up, you

discover your switchblade at your feet. Denny tips his head toward the rear of the great room. Barbara leads the way to the bookcases. She steps over Vincent's legs to do it.

The Boss is slumped against a wall. His shirt is so bloody, it's sucked to him. The old guy is still alive, but the way he looks up at you, you wonder how many of you he sees. He gives you a brave half-smile and closes his eyes.

You don't look back. "Lily? *Lily!*"

Barbara slides the bookcase back to reveal the panic room's steel door. Barbara knocks three times. "Open up! It's me!"

Two locks click open. Lily peers out, her eyes wet. Tears stream down her cheeks as she points behind her. She dragged Pete in there in the confusion of the Romanians' attack, but Pete's just a heap on the floor now. His eyes are open. Even in death, his eyes are shark's eyes.

Lily's cool hands clasp your face and you pull her to you. Your hearing is recovering. That distant screaming is Jimmy Lima. He must have fallen through the floor as his castle walls collapsed. He's screaming that his legs are broken.

Barbara covers her ears and leans into Denny. You knew Jimmy was mean, but in her face you see yourself the night you killed Tia Marta. Barbara has no pity or regret left for her husband. All that's left for Jimmy's demise is...relief?

"That screaming will make it easier for the Romanians to find him through the smoke. Don't worry, Barbara. They won't let the fire take him. They'll want the satisfaction."

There's more gunfire. It sounds like it's coming

from behind the house.

You grab Lily's shoulder and pull, but Denny's big paw holds you back. He holds out the locker key. "Tómelo." *Take it.*

"You're sure?"

Denny grins. "The cops will be here soon. Barb was talking about redecorating, anyway. We'll stay. It was always the plan that she'd get the house in the divorce. Now we're going to get everything. And besides," he looks down at his leg and his shoulder wound, "I'm not up to running. Running is your thing."

You take the key. "Gracias. Sorry about the leg, bro."

"I should have trusted you about Barb, but you always cheated me on splitting the restaurant bills."

"You...The restaurant tabs? Really?"

"I can do math better than you think. If a dude will take me on the little things, I can't trust him with something as big as messing with the under-boss's wife."

You want to say something. There isn't time. Lily pulls you away and Barbara pulls Denny into the panic room. The door slides closed and the locks click.

You've thrown a brother away again.

THE GARAGE

A couple of the *Banda,* Ion and Mihai, are waiting for you in Jimmy Lima's underground garage. Before you can say anything, Mihai, the tall black-bearded Romanian who wired the Semtex, claps you on the shoulder. "Jesus!"

"I told you, it's pronounced, *Hay-soose.*"

"Sure. Big bang boom, huh?"

"You have no idea."

Ion, looking amped up, steps from behind Mihai. He carries an Uzi and you wonder if he got it from one of Jimmy's fallen guards. He gives you the fish eye. You're glad you have the SIG tucked into the back of your waistband so your hands are empty and he can't take anything you do as a sign of aggression.

Mihai gives you a broad smile. "The *Banda* thanks you for your help. You did the right thing. Boss Cob and his children will rest in peace."

"You're welcome," you say. "The ride I came in on is a jigsaw of thousands of tiny pieces. I need one of Jimmy's cars. It won't be long before the cops are on the way. We made too big a bang boom."

Mihai laughs and points you toward a sporty

Toyota. "Yeah, we gotta finish our business and get everybody out. The keys are in it, Jesus." Behind the Toyota is an older model Ford sedan.

You tear open the Toyota's driver's side door and yell at Lily to jump in. You climb behind the wheel. In your rearview mirror, you catch Ion and Mihai running for the far side of the garage. Lily's cool hand covers yours as you're about to turn the ignition.

You duck your head. A green and blue wire snakes out under the steering column and disappears under the dash. "Sons of bitches! The Romanians had a little bit of Semtex left over. Just enough to blow us back to a basement in Florida."

"What?"

"Never mind. We're about to conduct a science experiment to see how stable Semtex is." You reach under the dash and rip the wires free. "Put your seatbelt on." You pause and hand Lily the blue and green wires. "Better keep your head down and hold these wires apart, okay?"

Ion yells out to you from the darkness. "Go! Go! The police will be here soon! We're clearing out in a few minutes!"

You roll down your window. "What?"

Ion steps out into view. "I said — "

You gun the engine and, to Ion's disappointment, you're still here. Ion's face snaps shut into a grimace of hate and frustration and he's pulling the Uzi up as you slip into reverse and press the accelerator into the floorboard. The Toyota jumps backward. Ion raises his weapon to take you out but hesitates when he realizes that even if he shoots you in the head, the momentum of the car will still run him down. That moment is all you need. He leaps to the side, you twist the wheel and slam his body into a pillar. The thug is pinned upright at the waist. The shock doesn't take him. Instead, he screams.

You roll out of the Toyota and come up into a crouch and raise the SIG. You put Ion out of his misery with one shot through his forehead.

Mihai rises up behind the Ford. He doesn't have time to reach for the Beretta in his shoulder holster. Your aim is already locked on the center of his chest. You take the Beretta from him and hand it to Lily. She holds it as if you just handed her a full ashtray.

"Mihai," you say, "I'm having a pretty bad day, man."

"Mine's worse," he says. He puts his hands high over his head.

"Why? We had a deal."

He shrugs, staring at your pistol as if, through sheer concentration, he can transform it into a wad of cotton candy. "A guy like you? An enforcer who can turn his back on his own people? You did the right thing helping us avenge the children, but...it was decided."

"That makes no sense. You knew I was getting out, anyway."

Mihai shrugs. "Clean slate. A guy like you — "

"Yeah, a guy like me.... The best friend I ever had just told me in not so many words that I'm a piece of shit a few minutes ago. Turn around and get on your knees."

Mihai does as he's told, but he asks, trying to get in one last dig, "Was Denny wrong?"

"There were...circumstances, but no, he's not totally wrong." Then you see the double-cross. "I didn't say it was Denny."

"Um…"

"You called me *Jee-zuzz*. You don't think I know a Judas by now?" You stick the SIG's barrel along his cheek so he can hear its cold mouth whisper promises of a dark future. "What was Denny going to give you?"

"Expansion into New Jersey and no more competition from The Machine there."

"What else?"

"Nothing else."

"You ever see *Cop Land* with Sly Stallone? Serious movie. He's a half deaf sheriff."

"I've got nothing to tell you!"

"A gunshot next to Sly's ear — *this* close, Mihai — almost deafens him. Bursting an eardrum? I'm told it hurts so much you just wish someone would do you the favor of shooting you in the head so it's over. *What else*?"

Mihai spits on the concrete and shrugs. He's an old soldier, but even the code of silence can't matter that much to a guy who's about to be executed. "Denny called us right after you left with Vincent's car. Denny's going to be The Machine's new boss. He made a better deal. He said as soon as you are dead, he'd tell us where to find a storage locker stuffed with money as a bonus."

"I'm very disappointed, Mihai."

He chances a look back at you and says, "Denny could have let you walk away. We didn't care as long as we got Jimmy and Vincent Lima. New territory and less competition from The Machine, respecting boundaries…that was more than we expected. You think Big Denny's your best friend? You really *must* be a piece of shit, huh, Jesus?"

You glance Lily's way. Her wide, wet eyes tell you this is too much for her. You've got to get her out of here.

"Mihai, I'm going to prove to you that I'm not as bad a guy as you've been told." You turn the SIG over in your hand and bring the butt down on the spot behind his ear as hard as you can. It takes a few swings, but after some flopping around, he's finally out.

"Christ, Jesus!"

"Relax. He's not dead. He's got a concussion. He might not be able to do long division any time soon. Explaining to the cops why he's here will give him a wicked headache. By the time he gets out of jail, that beard's going to be long and white. Let's go."

But Lily doesn't move. "He tried to kill us. You killed his buddy. He'll come after us. Or he'll send somebody after us from jail. Why didn't you kill him?"

Mihai is already coming around, moaning. His fingers touch his skull and come away bloody, but he's feeble, dazed and no threat now.

"I don't want to be the guy Denny knew, Lily. I want to be the guy you want to know. I'm going to be the guy who studies art with you in Spain and Paris. I'm going to be the good guy, babe."

"You're not." Lily raises Mihai's Beretta and shoots him in the head. His body shudders and is still. She keeps firing until the pistol clicks empty. The Romanian's head is a bowl full of salsa.

THE MAN YOU ARE NOT

Lily tosses Ion's Uzi into the Ford's back seat and puts the Beretta to your head. Sirens wail in the distance. "Get us out of here!"

It will probably be firefighters who arrive first, but a properly executed getaway would be a great idea, preferably at least several minutes ago. There's a little business to be taken care of first.

"You don't need that," you say, but Lily can only hear the sirens. "Put the gun down, Lily."

"What if I — "

You grab the barrel and push the slide back while twisting the Beretta upward. Trapped against the trigger guard, her index finger is pulled back painfully. Lily's shoulder drops until the muzzle points at her face.

"What if I say no? What if you shoot me in the head? I'd still love you. Don't you get it? I fucking *worship* you, Lily! You don't need a gun with me." As soon as she lets go of the Beretta, you twirl it around and give it back to her. Then you give her the storage locker key. "Got it?"

"I got it solid. Please, let's go." Lily sits back

against the door and you gun the engine. She leaves the Beretta in her lap and pushes back in the passenger seat, bracing herself. No big bang boom through your temple. It would sap energy from your chivalry to point out that the Beretta is empty, so you keep that to yourself.

The Ford shoots out of the back gate and the tires squeal in protest as you twist the wheel and head toward the city. The gate's hanging open and Freejack Jack's car is gone. How many of The Machine's guys got away and how many will come back? The Machine is made of a couple of hundred associates: punks, wannabes, overseers, loan sharks, bookies, regular muscle, fronts, lawyers, enforcers and the thirty-five higher-up, made soldiers. Denny's got about the same number as the DeCavalcante crime family used to have in Jersey: about a hundred guys. The DeCavalcantes thought *The Sopranos* was based on them and a lot of guys thought they might be right. Denny will be a real threat once he reorganizes. Unlike the DeCavalcantes, The Machine will carry on. Now is the time to disappear.

"Why didn't Denny kill you himself?" Lily asks.

"Old time's sake."

"No, really."

"I'm on his to-do list, sure, but he's safe up in the panic room with no gunpowder residue on his hands. When the cops show, they'll take everybody left alive to jail, but he won't stay there long. Jimmy's lawyer is also Barbara's lawyer so he'll have high-powered legal muscle on his side. He'll just be the big guy on crutches comforting the widow as far as the cops can prove."

"So Denny will be after us, too? Really? Why won't

he go to jail?"

"The lawyer will just say he was in the wrong place at the wrong time, that he was Mrs. Lima's bodyguard or something. That's what I'd do if I were him. Play dumb. All this time…I think Big Denny was pretty good at playing dumb. Nobody knows what goes on in anybody else's head, I guess. All this time, I thought I was the ninja."

"So Denny's really going to walk? That's bad for us, Jesus."

"He'll limp, but yeah. The cops will know the score but they'll call today a victory over organized crime, anyway. We kill each other and the cops pat themselves on the back for a job well done. They'll be very happy Vincent and Jimmy Lima are dead. With Pete and Bob gone, it leaves a power vacuum, but not for long. Five minutes, maybe. The Fed's anti-drug task force will throw a party with strippers and blow this weekend. It's quite a week for them, but before they're over their hangovers, The Machine will be back in business and allied with the *Banda* now."

You check the rearview mirror and realize you're making a rookie mistake. You're speeding away from a crime scene. You ease up on the gas pedal and drive a few miles over the speed limit like a normal citizen.

"What happens next?"

"When The Machine comes back, Denny will step in and be an important guy. When he double-crossed me, he bought a truce and standing with the *Banda*, though maybe not as much if we have Panama Bob's skim."

Lily opens the glove box and finds a pack of cigarettes. She puts the Beretta in there, too, and your shoulders relax as a ladder truck and a water truck scream past, heading to Jimmy's castle. It's Barbara's home now, be it ever so bombed, aflame, water-damaged and humbled.

Vincent made a classic military error: He underestimated his enemies. He didn't pull in all his available numbers from the streets to defend his perimeter. He thought he'd get another afternoon of earning out of The Machine before the war began. It's a common flaw: The arrogance of a smart guy who gets too comfortable. That attitude killed Vincent and it almost killed you. In *The Godfather*, Michael never got comfortable so he got to live, though he wiped everyone out until he ran out of friends.

In *Apocalypse Now*, Martin Sheen's soldier knew that every minute he stayed in his hotel room, Charlie was getting stronger out in the jungle. You let yourself be weak. You didn't see what was happening beyond the day-to-day bullshit. You had no idea Denny was banging Jimmy's wife. You didn't find a way to get out from under the shit assignment of whacking Panama Bob. Bob was right all along. Out on the ledge, hiding behind a gargoyle, Bob told you that the first thing they do in a conspiracy is kill the assassin. You let Denny get stronger while you dreamed on about the skim like a stupid lottery player. You are not a smart ninja.

"What are you thinking about?" Lily asks.

"Movies."

"I'm thinking about my father."

"Right. Sorry about Pete."

"Yeah." Lily's quiet for a long time. "You know those prints on my wall? The Dalis?"

"The melting clocks guy and the other one?"

"Salvador Dali. The artist's name is *Salvador Dali!*"

No idea why she's so pissed, you shut up and wait, keep your gaze on the road, and keep glancing in the rearview mirror, alert for bad news.

And Lily tells you about Salvador Dali's life. "He thought he was the reincarnation of his dead brother. He was as old as I am now when he illustrated his first book. He dressed weird and acted weird, but he could paint. People know all about the melting clocks, but before that he messed around with Cubism. He could paint anything. It didn't have to be strange, but he had to be different. Some of his paintings are floating around with forged signatures. Dali sometimes got his chauffeur to sign his paintings for him. It made him laugh to think of rich people paying big bucks for his paintings, putting it on their walls and saying 'There's the master's signature!'"

"That's kind of a cool 'fuck you.'"

"You'll like this part, Jesus. Dali experimented with Bulletism."

"He shot at a painting or something?"

"He'd shoot paint at paper and develop an image out of the ink blot."

"Okay."

"He even lived in his own museum! He was crazy, but genius crazy, not the regular kind of crazy like the guys in The Machine. Not like guys like you."

You turn that over in your mind. You don't like where this is going. "We can get away and live a different life. We can reinvent ourselves. I've already done it a couple of times. I started out as a swimmer, shit happened, I got in the Army, I got out — ”

“And you got into another army. You didn’t change, Jesus. Wherever you go, you’ll always drag a heavy bag of bad behind you.”

You stop at a red light and dare to look over at her for the first time. Black mascara slides down her cheeks.

“You’re a great salsa dancer, Jesus, but that’s not enough,” Lily says. “I want to be crazy like Salvador Dali. I want to live a big life, live long, and when I die, I want to inspire a bunch of bitches I never met to say they want to live like I did. If I go with you, all we’ll do is hide. I don’t want to live my life in hiding, Jesus. I want to live a big, Salvador Dali-sized life.”

You swallow hard.

She talks some more, but you aren’t really listening for the meaning of her words anymore. Instead, you listen to her soft accent, memorize the musical rise and fall of her voice and breathe in the faint hint of lavender. No matter where you go, you will always have a bottle of lavender with you as a reminder. Part of Lily will never get away.

You say, “I’ll drop you off at the locker.” You mean, *“Please don’t leave.”*

When she steps out of the car, Lily doesn’t look back.

THE MAN YOU ARE

You slip around the "Restroom Closed for Maintenance" sign and climb the steps two at a time. The Post Office's second floor is the perfect observation post to surveil the storage locker business. You didn't know for sure the federal agent would be there, drinking coffee and peering through a camera with a huge zoom lens, but it's the obvious spot for a lookout. The fed wears a sweater vest over a blue buttoned-up Oxford shirt and Mom jeans. If that weren't enough of a clue, the baseball cap that reads FBI in bright yellow stitching confirms all you need to know.

"Agent! There's a *gorgeous* Latina moving in on the objective! Have you spotted her yet?"

"Wha — ?" The guy looks up and that moment of indecision between reaching for his weapon and reaching for the walkie-talkie is plenty of time to whip the Uzi out from under your trench and smack him across the face with it. He's knocked against the wall and face down on the floor before he can get to the *t* in "What?"

You grab the walkie-talkie. "All units, stand by. Do

not move in. Keep this channel clear. Over."

When you handcuff his wrists, they make a satisfying ratcheting sound. You should have been a cop. In retrospect, that would have been a better career choice. Who knows? You could have been the guy on the floor with the swelling jaw.

"Nice sweater vest. What's your name?" you ask.

He says two words. The second word is "you." The first word is not "thank."

You fish his ID out of the FBI jacket hanging from the camera tripod. "Agent *Smith*?"

"You are in for a world of trouble, mister."

You have to chuckle. The guy sounds like a high school principal, not a supercop.

You read his home address to him off his driver's license. That settles him down immensely. That, and saying, "Sh!" while putting your SIG to his head.

You key the walkie-talkie's mic. "This is Smith. The Latina going for the storage locker. Do not move on her. Do not move on her. Maintain radio silence. Over."

"That won't work," Smith says.

"Your name is Agent *John* Smith? Really? Agent *Smith*? I suppose it's a common name for a white guy, but your buddies must have made a lot of *Matrix* jokes about you when the movie came out, huh?"

"Yeah, they did, but I haven't heard a *Matrix* reference in months. Listen — "

"Is this the part where you tell me we're going to be besties? Let me guess: If I put the gun down, give you back your driver's license and forget your address, we'll go around the corner to Saluggi's. We'll share a pizza pie and a few laughs, right? Bad things happen to my friends, man."

The radio crackles. "Smith? Come in?"

You key the radio and just say, "Stand by." Thanks to Tia Marta and her insistent elocution lessons, you sound like a white guy to the FBI.

"They are going to be all over you in a minute."

"How'd you find the locker? How long you been on this stakeout?" He doesn't say anything until you ask, "You got a wife and kids up there in Elizabeth, New Jersey?"

"There was a body in the locker. Shot in the head." Smith says. "It was wrapped up, but the smell still got out and the owner of the lot called the police. I've been on this stakeout for about a week.

So that's what happened to Cat Fornes. Panama Bob Lima shot him. Cat was a tough guy, but nobody's tougher than a bullet that's worth about two bits and no amount of sit-ups makes anyone immortal. Old Bob was tougher than anyone thought.

"You the shooter?" Smith asks.

"Nah, but you can close the case with this: Big Denny De Molina did it. Take it from me. In fact, I'm here on Big Denny's behalf, so when you start with your chasing and beating, start and end with Big Denny De Molina."

"You still talking? Sounds like a lot of hot air," Smith says.

You can't help but smirk. "Yeah, I get that a lot. You need evidence. You know who Denny is because you know who Jimmy Lima is. Jimmy's dead. Get a warrant for his records. Somewhere in the paperwork for one of his legit businesses, a property management company, is the money trail for pay that goes to Denny De Molina. He's listed as the Assistant Super and his rent is free. Denny could break a toilet by sitting on it, but he sure wouldn't know how to fix one. Then get a warrant for the Assistant Super's residence, Apartment C, in the basement. There's a big freezer that doesn't work. You'll find a lot of explosive residue there and some very illegal firearms. That should give ATF something to get excited about."

"Interesting. Anything else?"

"That'll be a good start."

"If you're here for him, what have you got against the guy?"

"Family feud. And I don't want to have another family reunion any time soon." That ought to keep everybody busy for a little while, at least.

You look through the camera. The old guy up front at the storage facility's office is peering toward you holding a walkie-talkie. Lily thinks she's talking her way to the storage locker and getting by on her looks and charm. The agent would let in anyone with a key to locker 408. In is easy. The trick will be getting her out.

You angle the camera and zoom in. There's the lovely Lily. She unlocks the padlock, bends to pull the metal door and it slides up. It probably still smells bad in there. Otherwise, the Feds would have a guy in there waiting to arrest her. If you don't do something drastic soon, the rest of Smith's stakeout team will ignore your walkie-talkie antics and put her in cuffs. Handcuffs aren't the sort of bracelets she's destined to enjoy. She's going to study art in France and Spain.

Lucky for Lily Vasquez, lover of Salvador Dali, ex-lover of the loser you have been, it's new leaf time. You take Smith's pistol and his FBI cap and sling the trench over the Uzi to hide it.

Lily comes out of the locker with two suitcases, one in each hand. The old agent from the booth moves toward her. You smash out the bathroom window with your elbow, stick the SIG out and fire two shots into the air. The old guy wheels and dives for cover.

Good luck, Lily.

The walkie-talkie crackles. "Johnny? What's going on up there?"

"This is Mr. Anderson," you say. "I have an automatic weapon pointed at Agent Smith's head. Pull back and let the girl go or I will blow his stupid head off."

"Anderson? Who are you?"

"Don't you remember Mr. Anderson? Code name Neo? Keanu Reeves played me in the *Matrix* movies. I'm Agent Smith's nemesis. Pull back and let the girl go with her suitcases or I will kill your man. Guaranteed. No kung fu. Just *bang!*"

There's some cross chatter on the channel as the FBI crew regroups to figure out what they're going to do. You're hoping embarrassment will slow their response, but you've learned your lesson: Never underestimate the enemy. SWAT's surely already on its way. On the other hand, SWAT will be way too late. You have no idea how many guys the FBI would spare for a stakeout like this, but not enough to set up a perimeter quickly enough.

"I should kill Agent John Smith just for his fashion sense. If you're going to carry a gun, you can't wear a sweater vest. Make a choice. The shirt's okay, but I don't know if I can forgive the pussy sweater vest."

"Hold on!" It's got to be the old agent pretending to be the storage locker guard. He'd have to be the senior agent on the stake out. "Don't do anything crazy! Let's talk about this before you do anything you can't take back."

"I'm already ten past crazy o'clock." You mute the walkie-talkie and slide it under your trench just as three guys with FBI emblazoned in yellow across their backs race across the street and up the Post Office steps. They pass you without giving you a glance. In their rush to be heroes, they're focusing on the wrong details. You empathize. You've done that.

Once they're out of sight, you raise the walkie-talkie and key the mic, "Back off or I'll kneecap your boy!"

Sirens wail, coming fast, but you're already a block away by the time they figure out you aren't in the observation post with Agent Smith.

You cross Canal street and slide up beside Lily. "The FBI will be after you. The money will be real so they have evidence but there have to be tracers in there. Grab a cab uptown and as soon as you can, get those suitcases underwater. A fountain, a bathtub, a hotel swimming pool. Whatever it takes. I'll draw them off and stall them."

"How'd you know that would work? I saw the guy coming toward me with his gun out as soon as I came out with the suitcases."

"Han Solo tried to bluff the Stormtroopers when he and Luke Skywalker rescued Princess Leia from the Death Star's jail. He tried to bluff, but Han didn't have my gift of gab."

"I guess not." Her eyes are wide and shining.

Before she can turn away and hail a cab, you kiss her for the last time.

As you steam away, you turn up the volume on the walkie-talkie and tell the feds if they leave the Post Office, three cars on the block will explode.

Smith answers immediately, "You son of a bitch! When I find you, you are going down so hard. We don't believe a word you say, you fucking piece of shit liar! You can't sucker us twice!"

"Three cars, pigs! Just like the Cutlass Supreme that exploded outside of Jimmy Lima's house this morning in Great Neck! Three cars wired with Semtex just like that one. I'll detonate them one at a time, killing civilians up and down this busy block. Try me, Sweater Vest! One explosion for every FBI jacket I see."

The key to a great bluff is specifics, conviction and evidence you've already taken the full tour of Crazy Town. You drop the walkie-talkie into a garbage can and keep going.

When you glance back, Lily's already in a cab, going away and getting away. Soon she'll be just a dot on the horizon. Then less than a dot. Then just a memory.

To her, you were always and forever going to be nothing more than the salsa dancer she had fun with for a while on her way to Dali. As you head down Greene Street, you promise yourself that, as good a liar as you are, you'll never lie to yourself again.

But how can anyone know when they lie to themselves and when they do not? Maybe you're lying again right now. Every day you talk to yourself. There is no "I". There is only "you." You have to be your own friend. Talking to yourself, separating the pained, tortured "I" from the cool, smart ninja "you"? That's what got you through the hell that was Tia Marta and The Bug Man's basement prison and every bad thing that's happened since.

You spot a cab and make a run for it. You don't see any FBI agents chasing you. "They better not," you tell yourself, "With a gun in your hand, nobody's bigger than Jesus."

Look for the next instalment in
The Hit Man Series:
Higher Than Jesus
By Robert Chazz Chute

About the Author

After several years working in the publishing industry, I took a long hiatus and then founded Ex Parte Press. I was a journalist and magazine columnist and now write in a lead-lined bunker full-time. I'm happily chained to my writing desk by an intravenous line feeding me espresso. My desk chair is a toilet and I'm writing as fast and as well as I can.

Thank you so much for reading **Bigger Than Jesus**. If you liked it, it will help Jesus Diaz and me immensely if you could please leave a happy review on Goodreads or Amazon or wherever you bought this book. Watch for the next instalment in this series: **Higher Than Jesus,** coming soon. Five books are planned for this series so far. If you'd like to get a glimpse of Jesus as a mature, more professional hit man, you can find the story that started his character in my collection of short stories, *Self-help for Stoners*. You'll find he's more polished, but things still go awry. All the latest updates about my books can be found at AllThatChazz.com.

Better yet, subscribe to my mailing list there. I won't pester you, but I will let you know about contests, prizes and when new books are available.

Discover other titles by Robert Chazz Chute
Higher Than Jesus
Murders Among Dead Trees
The Dangerous Kind & Other Stories
Self-help for Stoners
Sex, Death & Mind Control (for fun and profit)
Crack the Indie Author Code
Write Your Book: Aspire to Inspire

**For more information about me, my books and the All That Chazz podcast, please visit me at my blog:
www.allthatchazz.com**

**Fellow writers may also enjoy my writing blog:
www.chazzwrites.com**

* * *

**Follow me on Twitter:
@rchazzchute**

**For media requests, requests for
speaking engagements and to provide
feedback, please email me at:
expartepress@gmail.com**

Thanks again!

www.ingramcontent.com/pod-product-compliance
Lightning Source LLC
Chambersburg PA
CBHW050003070726
47592CB00018B/354